Blitz Bullion Busters

Daryl Joyce

Clink
Street

Published by Clink Street Publishing 2022

Copyright © 2022

First edition.

ISBNs:
978-1-915229-21-2 Paperback
978-1-915229-22-9 Ebook

To the real Mrs Poppet, wherever you are.

1

Wade Carter had made it all the way past the police van without being seen. He crouched down and could see the small dog rapidly making its way towards a ring of white posts with '*Police – do not enter*' tape around the perimeter. If they saw him, he'd be hung, drawn and quartered.

Keeping low, he reached the edge of the large hole by some piles of earth, trying to entice the dog to him. The little dog was running around the other side of the hole, some three metres away, begging for more of the chasing game. Wade investigated the hole. What he saw though was terrifying – the policeman had not been lying. Around a metre down was a long, rust-encrusted dark object. For some reason, he half expected to see the word *Bomb* written on its side and hear a loud ticking. *Is that really a bomb*? thought Wade. The rounded end and tailfin gave no doubt as to what it was. He backed away very slowly, caught up in the moment.

The dog yapped and ran around him and back to the other side, clearly enjoying this new freedom. Wade thought for a second, before putting his hand in his pocket and pulling out his lunch. He threw the meat paste sandwich over the hole at the dog, who briefly sniffed it before gobbling it. The dog ran to Wade and begged for more. Wade put his last sandwich in the dog's mouth, then grabbed him and ran as fast as he could back to the police van. The dog struggled but continued to be more interested in chewing than escaping. Fifty metres away he could see the elderly woman and the policeman still talking. He was glad that the policeman was facing the other way, as he silently arrived back at the barrier. Suddenly the policeman turned to his left to see Wade standing there, both he and the dog chewing.

'What the hell are you doing there?' said Constable Mirabelle loudly and suspiciously.

'Me, sir? Nothing, sir.' He put the dog into the old woman's arms. 'The dog just ran back to me as I stood here doing nothing, so I gave it my lunch.' Constable Mirabelle looked back along the path towards the van and park, then back to Wade. He was about to speak, when his thoughts were disturbed by another police van driving towards them, silent but with blue lights flashing.

'Right, well move along all of you please,' Constable Mirabelle said as he shepherded them further back, 'and take your little doggie with you.' The old lady smiled and stroked her dog vigorously.

'Oh, you're a wonderful little man. You rescued my little *Oro Fluffikins*!' She looked at Wade with glassy eyes and shook his hand as ferociously as she could for someone over eighty years old. Wade smiled back at her, shrugging his shoulders in an 'ah it's nothing' type of way. *Oro Fluffikins?! Poor dog* he thought. He was also wishing that he had not given all his lunch to that yappy little dog. He looked at his watch; he was already late for school.

Wade squeezed through the small gap in the school fence and bolted across the senior playground. He looked through the grimy windows of his classroom and saw his teacher talking to the rest of the class. They were all sitting down with coats on and bags on desks, ready to leave for their trip to the War Museum. Breathing a sigh of relief, he covertly slipped into the classroom and sat down next to his best friend – a relieved-looking Jack.

'Thought you weren't coming, Wadey,' whispered Jack.

'Try and stop me!' he panted. 'You won't believe what happened to me this morning – in the park was this World War Two UXB –'

'Mr Carter,' came the commanding voice of Mrs Poppet over the top of the class, 'you're already late. Don't make it worse by forgetting your manners.'

'No, Miss, it wasn't my fault, there was a bomb in the park and –' he stopped as the class gave an audible groan.

'Really, Wade, another tall story? Honestly, you come in here every day with amazing tall tales of your incredible life! I recommend, for your own well-being, that you're quiet for at least the next ten minutes.' Wade was about to speak, but he felt Jack's hand on his coat sleeve. He closed his mouth mid-word and turned to face Jack, who gave a weak smile.

Mrs Poppet checked to make sure everyone knew the routines and asked if there were any more questions. After a few seconds, one boy put his hand up.

'Miss, do you think they will let us fire guns and fly a Spitfire?' There was another groan from the rest of the class.

'Justin,' began Mrs Poppet, 'Justin... go to the front of the line. Everyone else line up behind him.'

2

'No, really – I rescued a dog from a UXB!' Wade exclaimed to a slightly disbelieving Jack once they were on the bus.

'Well, there *were* a lot of bombs that fell here during the war I suppose,' chipped in Jack. Wade harrumphed, as Jack continued; 'There could be dozens still undiscovered. In the Blitz, they reckon over 30,000 of them fell on London in the first three months!'

'Yes and I almost got blown up by one of them,' insisted Wade. 'How come you know so much about it?'

Jack smiled. 'It's my great-great-grandad Albert – he knows way more than me about the war and he's got all these souvenirs and stories! He once told me this time when he was a fireman in the Blitz and a building blew up next to him. He was blown across the street and as he lay there half alive, he saw a horse and cart driven by a ghost!'

'A ghost? On a horse?' asked Wade, amazed.

'Yeah, my great-great-grandad thought he was dead,' replied Jack, 'but the ghost rider and his horse just rode slowly by and disappeared.'

'Huh, we didn't need to go to the museum, we could have just got you and your great great-grandad to talk about it all!' Wade said nudging his friend. Jack stopped for a moment and nodded sagely.

'Jack, will you put away that aeroplane and you and Wade join the rest of the group.' Mrs Poppet peered over the top of her glasses and gave the boys that look – one of many that teachers master at teacher training. Jack quickly put the die-cast Spitfire back in his bag as he and Wade sheepishly joined the rest of their class. Their aged guide in this part of the museum was very enthusiastic. He continued.

'One of the strangest mysteries at the start of the war involved the theft of five hundred sixteen-ounce bars of gold from the Bank of England. At the time that was over £200,000 which may not sound much, but these days it would be almost seven million pounds!' There was an audible gasp from the assembled class. 'Yes, I thought that would get your attention, but maybe Colonel Bob can explain it better.' He paused and nodded at an unseen assistant. Behind him a film started.

Colonel Bob, a cartoon figure in the shape of a tank, explained that in September 1940 the government decided to move some of the country's gold to a more rural stronghold, away from the expected invasion. They secretly loaded it onto a guarded train at Bank to travel to London Bridge, where it would be taken by 'battle train' to an undisclosed location in the south of England. With the word *Reconstruction* in the corner, the film showed grainy black and white footage of trains, gold and soldiers.

'When it got to London Bridge, the gold was missing. No-one knew what had happened. Everyone was questioned – interrogated – but there were no answers. A crack team from New Scotland Yard was allocated to finding it, but no trace of it or how it disappeared was ever found. The man in charge was Inspector William Corner and he was still hunting for any trace of the gold on the day he was encouraged to retire in 1948.' The film juddered and on screen appeared the image of a weary police inspector. He was sitting on a seat in the middle of a large gloomy room with three men on chairs facing him. He spoke in clipped tones.

'Although my time on the case is ending, I have high hopes that we are close to a breakthrough and I know one day we will retrieve the gold.' The cartoon tank continued:

'The case was closed, unsolved, the day after Corner retired. No trace of the gold or who did it was ever found. There were all kinds of weird and wacky theories, from invisible Nazis to ghosts!'

Jack and Wade stared at each other wide-eyed for a moment. The cartoon character faded away and the aged curator continued;

'Fascinating mystery, eh? Does anyone have any questions?' He looked around and saw one child at the back frantically waving his hand. He signalled to him.

'Hello, I'm Wade Carter. My friend here – Jack Roble –' Jack looked at the ground, as Wade continued '– was wondering, why did they move the gold by train rather than the road?'

The curator widened his eyes and nodded. 'A good question, Wade, or Jack. Well, they wanted to make sure it was kept out of public view and public reach. Not panicking people was very important. It was simply much safer to transport it by Underground, rather than risk it being blown up or stolen. Gold is, and was, so very valuable. Desperate times led to desperate people led to desperate actions.' He nodded again sadly and saw the boy still had his hand up. 'Yes?'

'Hello, sir,' he began, 'I'm still Wade Carter and *my*

question is – well, I was wondering how much that gold weighed?'

'Wow, two good questions from one class – excellent!' The old man was clearly overjoyed now. 'Well one of the bars weighed sixteen ounces – I think you young people call it half of a kilogram in new money – so that would have been nearly two hundred and fifty kilograms. Very heavy indeed. As heavy as three teachers – just.' Wade looked impressed, although Mrs Poppet seemed less so.

'Don't forget we have a monthly competition. The prize is a trip to the RAF museum in Cosford and a ride in a genuine Spitfire!' There were a few gasps and hushed murmurs. Few heard him add the word 'simulator'. The curator continued; 'All you have to do is write how you think the gold disappeared and where it went to. The more imaginative and creative, the better! But remember, you've got to be original and true to life! Your teacher has the details. Get writing!'

'Thank you, sir. Now, are there any more questions?' said Mrs Poppet. Another hand shot up.

'Sir, I'm Justin – why didn't they just use the Internet to geotag it and locate it?' There was a loud groan from the rest of the class and Mrs Poppet pointed at Justin, then pointed to an empty floor space next to her. He walked over and sat down frowning. Seeing there were no more questions, the curator left and the teacher of 8P reminded them that they had thirty minutes to look around before they had to head back.

'Ah, I love all this stuff!' said Jack as he sped over to the 'Nazi's stole our gold' display. Wade sighed as he got up – he much preferred jumping over the tanks and guns on display in the main hall, although for some reason that was frowned upon.

3

As the 159 bus took them back to school, Wade had a far-away look in his eyes.

'Wonder where it went... Imagine what you'd do with a million quid of gold!'

Jack got the leaflet out and studied it. 'Says here that the train left Bank at 11:29 and arrived at London Bridge at 11:44, guarded by twenty soldiers. The gold had vanished from the carriage and no-one, not even the driver, could explain it. It had just vanished! Fascinating!'

'Oh, I bet you've worked it out – so who did it? That old man at the museum?' Wade laughed. Jack screwed up his eyes at the leaflet.

'What do you think that writing on that piece of paper means?' asked Jack. Wade took Jack's leaflet and looked at the small picture of the paper. It said '*SbnlBkSVBS24*'. Underneath it to the right were a few faint zig zag lines.

'Sabinnel-back-veebs-two-four?' Wade said slowly. 'Sounds like someone speaking backwards.' He grinned. 'Ah it's just all nonsense. Didn't they catch *anyone* to do with the gold going missing?'

'No, but it says here that the head of that department at the Bank of England – a bloke called *Sir Horatio Plum*

– was arrested, but there was no evidence. Then he died weirdly a few days later in the Blitz.'

'What's weird about that? I thought loads of people were killed with falling bombs and buildings falling down,' replied Wade, a little more interested now.

'Yeah, but he wasn't in his office, he was crossing a bridge in the middle of the night in an air raid!'

'Hmm, wonder why.' He screwed up his face. 'Oh well, rest in pieces!' They laughed most of the way back to school.

Once back in class, the teacher reminded them they could spend the final half-hour researching. With a grin, Wade and Jack wasted no time in heading to the Computer Suite. By the time they left an hour later, they felt like they had researched the whole Second World War and were carrying most of that research with them.

'Come back to mine and we'll work out what we've got!' Wade enthused as they left school.

The downside of Wade's life, he believed, was that he and his dad's world had been invaded by his new stepsister and her mum. They all had to live in a flat that you could barely swing a hamster in. Not that he owned a hamster, the council wouldn't allow it. He liked his new 'mum', but her teenage daughter – Faiza – just seemed to have it in for him. He used to have the second bedroom, but now she *had* to have that room. He was forced to have the 'cosy room'. That was another way of disguising the fact it was a broom cupboard. It was slightly larger than that, but he could only fit a small chest of drawers with a mirror and a bookcase around his single bed. It just didn't seem fair, Wade thought.

An hour later and Wade's room resembled the aftermath of a large explosion in a small paper warehouse. There were sheets of paper several deep on the bed, the bookcase and the drawers. No carpet was visible and both Wade and Jack looked a little forlorn. There were a few grey pictures and wordy descriptions of gold and other details of times and dates. They heard the telephone ring in the other room, followed by familiar footfalls. A few moments later, the door barged open and there stood Faiza.

'What's up, losers?' She walked in and flicked through Wade's grammar book. 'Need any help with your homework?' she added, as though she was talking to a five-year old.

'Get out Faiza, we're busy. Have you ever heard of privacy?'

'Yeah, I've heard of it,' said Faiza, 'and at least I can spell it.' She did one of those fake smiles. 'I was just watching the local news – they say they found a UXB not far from here in the park. Shame *you* didn't try and dig the door up!'

'Actually, I was there and I helped an old lady and her *Oro Fluffikins* –' said Wade proudly.

'Oh do shut up. Another tall story?' she sneered. 'Anyway, that was mum on the phone. She says she'll be back late tonight doing another shift and you'll have to do the kitchen.'

'Why can't you do it? I've got homework,' protested Wade.

'Yeah – you really look like you're working hard. Year Eight is so hard, right, especially if you're not very bright,' she said sarcastically. 'What happened here?' she snorted. 'Did your friend explode?'

Wade frowned as Faiza looked over at Jack with her head

tilted. 'You know, I'm still not sure your friend actually speaks. Is he real?' Faiza walked over to the drawers and picked up Jack's leaflet. 'Hey, the mystery of the gold that vanished – we did that when I was in Year Eight. My friend Janet said she thought that the gold was actually just painted ice and it melted and –'

'You know we really don't care. Just leave us alone.' Wade cut her off. She made that disinterested face.

'Well, don't forget the kitchen later, Squib. Just trying to help my little brother,' said Faiza, gently kicking his laundry basket.

'I'm not your little brother!' Wade shouted back. 'And I want my room back! Just get out!' He stood up. Jack just sat there, trying to be interested in the chest of drawers.

'You know what?' Faiza shouted, walking towards the door.

'What?' replied Wade, also with increasing volume. Faiza looked like she was going to shout something, but instead she paused and quietly said;

'One day, you'll realise I'm not the enemy.' She left the room, closing it quietly. Wade stood there for a few seconds with his fists clenched.

4

'I hate her; she's always trying to bring me down,' he muttered.

'You know, maybe she was just trying to be friendly,' Jack said quietly. 'She seems alright to me… bit scary maybe.'

'Scary? HA… no, she was after something. I know. She's big and scary and I have to give up everything so she can live here.'

'Well, that's not her fault,' Jack said quietly, 'and maybe she just wants to –'

'I know what *she* wants, but my dad has said that I must try. How come she gets *all* the good stuff *and* my room? And look – *this* is what I end up with.' He indicated the rest of his small room. 'She moved in here all big and smug and took my room and everything else!' Wade rounded on Jack. 'Why don't you let her move in with *you*?'

Wade sat down on the end of his bed kicking his laundry basket. Jack just stared at his friend for a few seconds, before pretending to be interested in his own feet. They stayed in silence for what seemed like hours. A minute later, Wade spoke quietly;

'Sorry.' He picked at an imaginary loose thread on his t-shirt. 'But sometimes it gets a bit…' He left the sentence unfinished.

'It's ok, bud,' Jack said, nodding slowly.

'Well, before you do move in with *her*, let's get this done. Right, I need the start sheet!' said Wade, trying to organise the paper into piles.

Jack produced a copy of the string of ten letters and two numbers that had been found in the tunnel by Bank Station.

'There it is!' said Wade snatching the paper from Jack. The paper seemed to be taunting them like it had countless others over for eighty years. '*SbnlBkSVBS24*'. 'So what does that two and odd-looking four mean then?' Wade asked.

'Well, interestingly, no-one knows for sure. Could be hours in a day or a unit of measurement?' Jack shrugged his shoulders.

'Yeah, I guess.' Wade repeated the string of letters several times. 'SbnlBk...?' It seemed familiar somehow. 'Anyway, based on all this information, just what have we worked out, *Inspector*?' asked Wade.

'OK here we go, *Chief*. One, the gold WAS on the train. It must have been on the train as no-one could have lifted all that gold away at Bank without someone seeing.'

'OK. Right, and?'

'Two – however the gold disappeared, it couldn't have just gone without people being in on it. Three – no trace of the gold was ever found, so it must still exist somewhere. And four,' Jack continued, 'Plum was arrested but never charged, and died a few days later on the bridge at midnight.'

'OK. What about other witnesses? There were plenty of people involved in moving the gold.' Wade grabbed some paper from a pile to his left and read from it. It was a statement from the driver, a man called Jeff, and even had a picture of him. He appeared like a 1940s train driver should be dressed; dungarees, cap, slightly dirty face and hands.

'He said that nothing happened on the fifteen-minute journey, and he didn't witness anything out of the ordinary,' said Jack.

'Oh well. So, no-one saw anything and no-one heard anything?' Wade asked, sighing.

'Well, we got rid of most of our first theories – the gold was not painted ice, the gold was not wax made into candles and it was not painted cake that the guards ate!' Both Jack and Wade laughed. 'And they didn't quickly make another carriage out of the gold!'

'What can we come up with that sounds like it could be true, *Inspector*?' Wade said impatiently.

'Our only working theory, *Chief*, is that Plum hid someone in the money carriage who threw the gold out the window for other people to catch. Then went back and got it before anyone went in the tunnel.'

'Come on, we'll never win with that one. How would they have got away with it?' Wade slumped down, suddenly feeling lost. Jack stared at the code thoughtfully.

'Let's start at the beginning – what were the two stations again?' asked Jack enthusiastically. Wade got out two bits of paper with the Underground on and they looked at them.

'Look – there's Bank station near the middle and there's London Bridge south of the Thames.'

'So, they put the gold on here at Bank and went south to London Bridge,' agreed Jack.

Something clicked in his mind. 'Wait a minute. South? Like southbound? Like Southbound from Bank to London Bridge?!' Jack looked at Wade who looked puzzled for a moment before he too shook his head.

'No, can't be. Where's that code? Where is it?!' They both excitedly scrabbled through the sheets of paper, looking briefly at each one. Eventually Jack picked up what they were looking for – the picture of a scribble and the code found in the empty money van. He held out the paper and looked at the scribble. '*SbnlBkSVBS24*'.

'That could be... could mean Southbound something Bank?'

'Ah yeah, it must do! But what about the other letters and numbers?' replied Wade excitedly. It went quiet, as both realised that they had no idea.

5

The door creaked open and in strode Faiza with a bemused look on her face. Wade seemed to be immediately on the defensive again.

'What do you want *this* time?' Wade dropped any pretence of friendship from his voice. 'We're doing something really important here, so if you don't mind…'

'Oh right, you're still working on the gold mystery thing… yeah, I heard you mention the southbound line from Bank,' she replied, picking up the piece of paper with the code on. 'Did you work out what the other squiggles were? My friend Janet thought they were a previous code scribbled out.' Wade looked at her, and then the piece of paper.

'Well, good for Janet. We thought that, obviously, but then we came up with a better idea,' Wade said eventually.

'And…?'

'It's a secret, isn't it, Jack?' They both looked at Jack, who just looked blankly back at them. Faiza's shoulders dropped, and her tone changed.

'Oh, I see. Well, Squib, dinner will be in a few minutes.' She glanced over at Jack. 'Guess you can stay too if you want.' Jack mumbled something and shook his head as she left. Wade just carried on sorting bits of paper.

'Still think she's nice?' Wade said to Jack, who just made a half-smile and looked at the code even more intently.

'Well, she –' started Jack.

'She's just nosey,' Wade said curtly.

'I would stay for dinner, but I'd better get going soon', said Jack. He decided to get back to the case in hand.

'If that *is* the southbound from Bank then,' Jack said, getting the Underground map. 'See that Bank station? Well, what do you see coming out of the station?'

'Erm – a red line and a black line,' Wade said and paused. 'Blimey – the Northern Line?'

'So then, have we now got – Southbound Northern Line Bank? Surely we can work out the key to the rest of it!' They both cheered. Suddenly Jack stopped wide-eyed.

'That's it!' Jack shouted. 'That's it!' He grabbed the piece of paper, looked at it and exclaimed: 'That squiggle of crossed out letters. It's not squiggles at all!'

'What is it?' Wade pleaded. Jack milked the moment, looking from Wade to the paper to Wade again.

'It's the design for a *key*!'

Wade grabbed the piece of paper with the squiggle on and held it up to the light, frowning.

'It is, it is!' Jack insisted. He got another piece of paper and drew it with a few less squiggles. 'Well, it's almost a key.' He handed it to Wade.

'Well, it could be – It looks very small. What would it open, a doll's house?'

'Hang on.' Jack picked up Wade's magnifying glass and peered at the original again. He had noticed that next to the 'squiggle' were some tiny symbols. He read them out; '1:4 DS.'

'Is that ratio? Remember that ratio lesson last month? Those two numbers are a ratio, each one is worth four.'

Wade's voice trailed off as Jack quickly redrew the key, muttering as he did so.

'Tadaah!' Jack held it up. Now it looked more like a long key, but still not quite right.

'I know – the DS is… look at the mirror – Double Sided!' said Wade proudly.

'Double Super!' exclaimed Jack. He reversed and repeated the pattern. He held up the new drawing of the key, now eight centimetres long with teeth on both sides. Wade and Jack laughed.

'Wow, you're almost clever!' Wade snatched the paper from him and held it up.

'I think we'd be cleverer if we knew what the key actually unlocked.'

Jack and Wade spent a few minutes trying to work out what the key could unlock, but the only ideas they could come up with were that it was the key to the secure gold carriage, the key to the station or the key to the driver's lunch box.

A shout from downstairs advised Wade that dinner was ready. They both made rushed attempts to tidy the paper into piles.

'What next then?' asked Jack excitedly.

'I guess we need to find out how to make a key? And then find out where the key fits!' said Wade.

'Look, let me keep this and I'll see what I can do.' Wade passed the diagram to Jack, who pocketed it and headed for the front door.

6

'I've done it,' Jack said to Wade as he strolled into Wade's room the next morning. Wade was in mid-munch, half-way through a bowl of cereal. In one hand, Jack held up a small, jagged piece of metal. It was greeny-grey and appeared to have part of a target painted on it. In his other hand, he held up the hastily drawn key diagram. Wade snatched it from him and turned it over.

'Wow. It looks amazing – where'd you get it from?' Jack reached into his pocket and pulled out the model Spitfire, now with one of the wings missing.

'I spent an hour last night cutting it up and I think it'll work.' Jack shrugged. 'But don't tell my dad, it's his model!'

'Well, that Spitfire will never fly again!'

'Maybe just in circles,' Jack replied. They both laughed.

'So how are we going to test out what the key fits, Inspector?' asked Wade.

'Well, Chief, I think we'll have to go to the scene of the crime,' replied Jack solemnly.

'Right, agreed. Let's do it,' announced Wade. Jack nodded; they had to go to the northern line platform at Bank and where it all happened. 'Even if it is over eighty years late!' Wade joked. One major obstacle stood in their way – something that children all over the world had to deal with daily; how to get past their parents.

'Dad…' Wade said to him downstairs a few minutes later. 'Got a problem…' Wade's dad finished doing his shoes up and peered at Wade.

'Money, friends, money, girls or money?' he quipped. Wade shuffled his feet and did his best innocent look.

'Ha ha, you're so funny, Dad. Really, really funny,' he said, 'but it's none of those. I've lost my phone – on the school trip.'

'Oh Wade.' He sighed. 'Have you tried ringing it?'

'Yeah, Dad. A man answered it and said he was at the office at the War Museum, where we went.'

'Well, I can't go and get it – I'm late for an appointment with the bank. You'll have to wait.'

'Well, Dad,' he smiled, 'I've got a great idea – I'll go with Jack and we can…'

'No, I don't think so…' Mr Carter shook his head and was about to list some reasons why not when Wade's new mum, Nida, came in with her coat on.

'Dexter, come on, we'll be late!' she said. Dexter briefly explained the situation. Nida thought for a few seconds.

'Look, why not let Wade go and get his phone,' Nida said, 'but Faiza can go with them.' Wade's smile turned to a frown.

'Good idea, love – there you go, Wade. All sorted, but be good mind,' he said, nodding. Wade tried to hide his dismay and started to protest, but Nida left to instruct Faiza. 'Listen, be nice to each other and here's a tenner for lunch if you and Faiza are out for long.'

'What's going on at the bank?' asked Wade, accepting the ten-pound note happily.

'Oh, we're just off to sort out a loan. Now look, you and

Jack be good for your sister and see you later,' he replied. They both left a few minutes later, leaving Wade a little thoughtful.

Jack came downstairs looking less happy than earlier.

'Yes, I heard – and I heard instructions to your sister to make sure we didn't get up to no good, and she was told to be nice to you too,' said Jack. Wade was about to voice his opinion, when Faiza came out of her room and into the lounge. Although her clothes gave the impression of being smart and ready, her face and hair said the opposite.

'Not a word, not a comment, not a look, Squib.' She looked at the two of them sitting there looking forlorn. 'Trust me, the last thing I wanted to do on a day off was babysit two *boys* around London.' She got an apple from the bowl and stared at them. 'Well come on then – we don't have all day. So, another trip to the War Museum?'

'Erm, no,' replied Wade, looking at Jack, 'We're going to Bank – that's where I remember having it last.' Faiza shrugged her shoulders. 'One more thing,' he continued, smiling. 'You gonna do your hair before we go?'

7

They arrived at Bank less than thirty minutes later via the Northern line from Stockwell. Faiza managed to keep her stern silence the entire journey, speaking in only single word answers when she felt the need. Wade got off the train, followed by a wide-eyed Jack and by Faiza, who also seemed to be curious about the whole place.

Once the train left, the place quietened for a moment before people continued shuffling onto the platform. It was warm and smelled lightly of oil, of people, and a little of old shoes. Faiza saw movement amongst the tracks and looked closer as small black things were scampering around the shadows. She stepped back; mice were not nice.

Wade noticed a man in a bright orange jacket looking at them slightly suspiciously – they were the only ones not heading somewhere.

'Can I help you?' he asked. Faiza was about to reply, when Wade cut her off.

'Erm, no thanks, Mr Tim...' he said, squinting at the '*May I help you*' badge, on which the last name was hard to read. 'We're just going.' He quickly headed through the small walkway connecting the north and south platforms, followed a few seconds later by Faiza and Jack.

'Hey, what's going on, Squib?' Faiza demanded, grabbing his coat.

'Well, I remembered that I left my camera somewhere round here.'

'I thought it was a phone?' Faiza was growing more impatient. Jack arrived, and she looked at both in turn. 'Well?'

'It was the camera on my phone.' Wade stopped and looked at Faiza's disbelieving face. 'OK, ok. It's not just my camera, or rather my phone. We needed to come here to…'

'What?! So, there is no missing phone? Oh, I don't believe it – you just wanted to come out and play!' she said with growing anger.

'No, well, no – you see, we think we managed to find some things out and I had to come here to Bank and…'

'Just wait till we get home and Mum hears about this – you're gonna be grounded forever!' She screeched in triumph. 'Even your dad won't be able to save you!'

'No, no, listen – it was all to do with that gold going missing – what your friend Janet was on about. I think we may have found some clues.'

'Clues about what? That missing gold from the war? What's that got to do with you and Captain Quiet?' Her volume had dropped a little, but she was still looking furious.

'Me and *Jack*.' He signalled Jack, who stood there with a pained expression. 'We figured out that the squiggle on the paper was part of a key and I think that it fits something here.'

'You and *him*?' She looked at Jack, then back at Wade. 'A key to what?' Wade put his hand out and Jack reluctantly handed him the metal key. Faiza snatched it and after looking at it for a few seconds, laughed loudly.

'It looks like a model airplane wing that's been caught in a blender. What's that supposed to fit? A train driver's lunchbox?' She laughed again.

'No, no, it's… look give us a chance. Just give us a few minutes and then we'll all go back home. What have you got to lose? You can grass me up then, but just give me a few minutes!' Wade pleaded. Faiza looked at them dubiously. 'And I'll give you my pocket money for the next month!' Faiza stared at him, and then the misshapen airplane wing for a few moments, before handing it back to Wade.

'Pocket money for the next month?' She paused thoughtfully. 'Go ahead then. I'm just going to wait exactly five minutes, then I'm going to laugh at you. Later, when you get grounded for ever, I'm going to laugh again, especially when you hand me money every week for a month!' She looked triumphantly at Wade and Jack.

Jack and Wade dodged around a few travellers and reached the far end of the platform. They scanned the walls, the ceiling and even the floor. There was nothing that a key would fit. They could both guess what Faiza was thinking, and it wasn't pleasant.

'This is turning into my best day ever!' she guffawed. 'Think we'd better head back to jail, don't you?' Wade's shoulders slumped a little, then he noticed that Jack was still on his knees.

'Jack, come on. We blew it,' Wade said, looking down at his friend. Jack meanwhile tugged Wade's trouser leg and pointed at the set of ceramic tiles at floor level. They were grimy and obscured by dust, but there in amongst the white and grey tiles were two small, tarnished brass plates. Under the two plates were a mixture of stencilled letters and numbers covered in a lot of dirt and dust. Wade bent down to see what his friend was so interested in and then sighed.

'It's just some metal plates with dusty letters and numbers,' moaned Wade.

'But it must mean something!' Very quickly, Jack reached into his bag and, using the metal top fin of the model aeroplane, tried to prise one of the plates off. With some effort, the fin eventually slid under a corner, and he was able to loosen it. It landed on the floor with a light clatter, as did the other one. Faiza meanwhile went from being cross to bemusement to genuine excitement. She knelt next to them, ignoring the grimy floor.

'What is it?' she whispered. 'What have you found? Is it gold?' All three of them stared at the small space where the plates had been. They could see two old plug sockets, but the pin holes looked larger and rounder.

'They're all gummed up with – ugh – stuff,' complained Jack.

'Looks like your bedroom,' muttered Faiza, before sighing and giving her hair clip to Wade. He passed it to Jack, who looked at it, and then at them and back at the hole, before grimacing and using it to clear it of dust and dirt.

'Now it looks like he's cleaning out your ears, Wade,' laughed Faiza. Wade ignored her.

'Hey that's great Jack – what's in there?'

'Too dark to see. Do you think,' said Jack pulling out his crudely fashioned metal wing, 'that this might fit it?' All three of them looked at it wide-eyed.

'Not sure you should stick that in there!' said Faiza with alarm.

A large hand landed dramatically on Faiza's shoulder. 'Just what is going on here?' demanded a voice.

Faiza and Wade turned around and stood up rapidly, followed a few moments later by Jack.

'Nothing, mister,' said Faiza with an innocent look, 'I was just doing my shoelace up and my friend here was trying to find some money he had dropped.' Mr Tim looked past them at the floor and the wall; he hadn't noticed that Jack had managed to put both plates back in place. He looked back at the three, who seemed to be looking around innocently. His features softened.

'Look, this can be a dangerous place, not a place for kids to hang around looking for trouble.'

'Oh, we're not looking for trouble, mister,' replied Faiza, doing her best 'girl-lost' act.

'Well, I'm afraid you've found it. Where are you going?' he raised an eyebrow.

'Bank,' blurted out Wade. The man nodded.

'You're in luck, you've arrived. So, let me escort you to the surface.' He urged them to move towards the stairs and exit, despite their protestations. Blinking in the sunshine, they were right outside the Bank of England. Looking at Mr Tim's determined face, there was no way they'd be able to get back in that way.

'Don't let me see you here again. I'll be watching,' he added, as if to confirm Wade's thoughts. They sheepishly crossed the road and headed down King William Street.

8

'Nicely done with the plates Jack,' said Wade. Jack shrugged his shoulders in a 'no problem' kind of way.

'Think your sister had a hand in it too,' said Jack quietly. A few minutes later they were sitting below London Bridge as the river flowed by.

'Still think we're idiots?' Wade said, with a hint of sarcasm – did he really want to tell *her* everything?

'Yep,' she replied, 'but you're idiots who may be onto something. What was down there?' Wade frowned, and silence followed 'You may as well tell me, else I'm off home and I'll get all your pocket money.'

'Well, it's like this,' started Jack, but was interrupted by an open-eyed Faiza.

'Wow, he really can speak! Go on – do it again!' she laughed.

'Ignore her, Jack, I'll tell her,' cut in Wade. He explained about the clues they had found so far and what their theories were. Faiza seemed a little disbelieving, but even she couldn't argue with the evidence. She took the paper from Jack and looked at the code and key pattern on it.

'So, you reckon the code so far means…?'

'Southbound Northern Line Bank… but what's SVB? And we don't know what the 2N4 means?'

'*Is* that really a four?' she asked no-one. The boys looked at it and shrugged their shoulders. It looked a lot like it, but the sloping part of the '4' was very faint. Wade looked at her.

'So, you gonna grass us up?'

'Might do. Depends if you, or rather *we*, find the gold or not.' She smiled that smug smile again. Wade knew he was beaten and that he would never get rid of her now, but then he guessed there were worse people to have around.

'How did Mr Tim know we were there?' asked Wade.

'CCTV.' Jack raised his eyes to one of the half a million CCTV cameras that cover London. He continued; 'They're everywhere.'

'He was probably first alarmed by your hair,' Wade said to Faiza, who frowned and pulled her hoodie up.

'Or by your gormless fancy-dress face,' she retorted.

'Well now what?' asked Jack, cutting them off.

'Well obviously, the first thing we need to do is get back down there and find out if Captain Quiet's key really works!' she said thoughtfully.

'But how are we going to get in if he's watching the entrances?'

They sat for a moment before Wade clicked his fingers. 'Got it – we walk to London Bridge station and get the train back to Bank!'

'Not bad, Wade,' said Faiza, as she got up, dusting herself down. They headed to London Bridge.

Back at Bank, they shuffled out amongst the crowd. There were still lots of people moving fast; many of them tutting for no real reason. Wade got to one end of the platform and turned on his heel and headed back the way he had come, mingling with the people. Jack shot out into the crowd and seemed to vanish. Faiza meanwhile headed to the opposite platform and did the same. A minute passed. And another minute. Still no-one noticed them.

Wade was just about to go and find Jack when there came a flash and a kerfuffle from the end of the opposite platform. There was a small crowd of people and a faint burning smell. Fighting his way through, Wade saw Jack sitting next to the wall looking a little dazed and there were small wisps of smoke coming from his hair.

'I found out what the code meant,' Jack mumbled, as he got to his feet and dusted himself down. Several of the passers-by asked if he was ok, but they waved them on.

'I managed to put the metal wing in the first socket when no-one was looking. Then there was a big bang, a big bright bang, and I ended up a few metres away. I can still see stars!' He laughed. Jack was holding the buckled wing of the Spitfire. Wade took it – it was warm to the touch – and put it in Jack's top pocket.

'Well I'm glad you're ok – I guess it was a bit stupid; must be live.'

'No kidding, Sherlock!' Jack smiled as Wade helped him to his feet. 'But yeah, it was more than a little stupid'

'Hang on – you said you knew what the code meant. So, what does it mean?' asked Wade.

'That 'four' isn't a 'four' – it's...' But Jack's explanation was cut short. A familiar figure in an orange jacket was forcefully holding Faiza. It was Mr Tim.

9

'Right, you three hooligans are coming with me. I'm calling the police. Get up. NOW!' Mr Tim bellowed at them, dragging Faiza. 'Just what the hell were you up to?'

'Just a mistake, Mr Tim, we got on the wrong train and –'

'Don't try it – go on, up you go.' He pushed them forwards, as other people parted to make way. On the left, on the way to the escalators, Wade stumbled over a small child darting around his parent's legs. Jack stopped to help him and noticed one of the large black and white floor tiles had a small, tarnished ring inlaid into it. Jack widened his eyes as he was pulled away – did it say SVB on it?

As they got to the top of the first set of stairs, Faiza stopped. They all looked at her as she doubled over.

'What's wrong, Faiza?' Wade asked. She looked up and winked at him.

'Come on, keep moving vandals,' shouted Mr Tim. Very quickly Faiza lifted her left foot and brought it sharply down Mr Tim's shin, landing it on his right foot. The effect was instantaneous; Mr Tim let go of Faiza and grabbed his foot. Wade took the initiative and barged into

Mr Tim. With a cry, the man went flying and landed with a thump and a shout.

'Run!' shouted Wade, and all three of them hurtled back down the escalators – fast. At the bottom of the escalator, Jack tried the ring in the floor tile, but it wouldn't budge.

'Meet me back here in three minutes!' he hissed, and they scattered. Behind them they could hear shouting getting closer. Mr Tim was no longer on his own and had called for backup.

Wade dodged around some tourists and ran along the corridor a little before sliding left into a small passageway. He ignored the tuts and teeth-kissing from some of the people he had to barge past. Pulling his jacket on and running further along the corridor, he saw he was heading for the Waterloo and City line. When he got to the end, Wade darted to the right behind the ticket barriers. The train was in the station and for a second, he considered getting on it but knew he couldn't abandon his friends. Wade put his head around the corner and saw Mr Tim at the far end of the corridor. To his horror, the man was coming his way.

Jack realised after a few seconds that Mr Tim had chosen not to follow him, which was a small relief. He reached the bottom of the escalator and once around the corner, he was back again near the two sockets. A man in a Hi-Viz jacket stood with his back to it and was on his radio. His way was blocked.

Faiza carried on down the next set of stairs and ducked down at the bottom of the up escalator. As one of Mr Tim's friends came hurtling down the other escalator, she headed upwards, unseen behind the other travellers.

At the top, near the ticket office, she quickly removed her jacket and queued at a ticket machine. Two large, out-of-condition men burst into view at the top of the escalator and looked around angrily. One pointed at the Lombard Street exit and bolted for it, whilst the other one began heading her way.

Wade knew what would happen if Mr Tim saw him, so he ducked around to the right and headed up the hundred-metre set of steps, which led away from the Waterloo and City line. Behind him at the bottom of the tunnel, he could just make out Mr Tim on his radio.

Jack was trapped. If he went back the way he had come, he was bound to meet his pursuers and if he went towards the sockets, the other man would see him. Just then, the man's radio crackled. Jack could hear the tinny voice shouting that one of them was on the escalators heading towards the Waterloo and City line. The man frowned and pressed the talk button;
'Charlie Tango, it's Colin – I'm on the southbound Northern line platform and I think they've got on the train that's just left.' He put his radio back on his belt. A few moments later, an excited voice spoke; 'Yes, I've tracked one to the Waterloo and City line – in pursuit!' Jack kept his head down as the man turned on his heels and ran towards and past him. Jack headed forward and didn't look back as he knelt in front of the sockets. He looked in his bag – where *was* the Spitfire wing?

In the ticket office, people seemed to make way for the red-faced man with little more than a frown. Faiza held her breath as he stopped near her. The radio attached to his belt crackled and he cocked one ear towards it. Faiza could make out the voice saying that they must have either got on one of the trains or somehow made it to the surface. The man pressed a button on the radio and said, 'Roger, on way.' He ran towards the exit marked 'Waterloo and City Line'. A few seconds passed and Faiza slowly breathed out. From where she was, she could see the mirrored glass of the security room. She looked away, imagining them all looking at her through the glass. She pretended very hard to look at a tube map leaflet, hoping that neither Wade nor his little friend had been caught.

A large, red-faced man ran in his direction, so Wade kept his head down and aimed for the ticket hall. The man looked determined as he ran past Wade. Trying to look like a tourist, Wade scanned the place, eventually spotting Faiza near the front of the queue for the ticket machine. Knowing it would be best if they weren't seen together, he brushed past her and headed through the barriers, towards where he hoped Jack would have solved their problems.

Was that her pocket being picked? Faiza turned and saw Wade now a metre or so away heading through the barriers. After a few moments and checking they weren't being followed, she used her Oyster to get through the barriers. It bleeped and lit up with 'Seek assistance'. She looked around nervously. A man in a yellow jacket looked over at her and signalled to come over.

Jack had searched his bag twice and was becoming desperate. Where was it? He looked up and saw a little girl eating an ice-cream whilst staring at him. The child was open mouthed and didn't notice some ice-cream had dribbled onto her shirt. Subconsciously Jack patted his shirt in the same place and then smiled! The key – Wade had put it in his top pocket! He pulled it out and, with a deep breath, he pushed the plane wing towards the second socket.

10

Jack half-closed his eyes – as if that would save him from an electrical jolt – and put the metal key in the top hole. Nothing. He pushed it further in and gingerly turned it. He thought he heard a distant switch or a clank, but nothing else. No explosion, no bang, no electricity. Was that right? He did it again and again. Nothing. Had he failed? He sat back puzzled. The small girl was still looking at him and now the child's parents were too. Jack stood up and backed away from them, towards the stairs. He must have failed.

Behind her, people mumbled as Faiza walked over to the yellow-jacketed man. He eyed her and put his hand out for her card. She handed it over gingerly, whilst looking past him where the mirrored glass seemed to be glaring at her. He took it and patted it on the gate sensor. After a long second, the gate opened. He smiled and ushered her through, mumbling something about a dodgy sensor. She whipped through the gate and was lost in the crowd on the down escalator.

Faiza had to say 'excuse me' seven times as she ran down the escalator. There she found Wade looking worried in the recess in front of a silver door. He was trying to look inconspicuous, but not managing it.

'Where's Jack?' she asked urgently. Wade shrugged. Suddenly, they heard some shouting way above them from beyond the top of the escalator.

'Stop them!' The shouts were getting louder, but people at the top just stopped and stared at the men trying to push past them. Behind Wade and Faiza, Jack reached the top of the other escalator and bolted towards them, pointing at the floor and shouting to pull the silver ring.

They needed no second telling – both Faiza and Wade pulled at the silver ring. It didn't move. Anxiously all three of them pulled it, using their combined might. Slowly and with a gust of stale air, it opened just a few centimetres. Jack wedged it open further as Wade, then Faiza, slipped through. Jack followed and they disappeared into the darkness. The tile closed shut above them with a gust of air and some clicks. Mr Tim and one of his 'friends' fought their way past the crowd to the bottom of the escalator. As though in a cartoon, they looked around, up the escalator and down again and at everyone. Mr Tim kicked the wall – somehow, they really had vanished!

11

The three escapees panted heavily in the darkness as they sat with their backs to a wall. They could hear footfalls on the floor above them and raised, but indistinct voices.

'Are we just the best or what? Did you see them come right after me?' Wade asked excitedly. In the darkness, Faiza tutted.

'I think I was the one they were after! I was right by them in the ticket office!' she boasted.

'I went all the way to the Waterloo and City line, whatever that is!' retorted Wade.

'Yeah, well, Mr Tim saw you and nearly got us all caught!' Faiza replied.

'Well I dodged him, didn't I? I bet he saw you first, you're way bigger.' Wade stopped mid-moan. Jack hadn't said anything since they got in there – in fact with it being so dark, they couldn't even be sure he was there. 'Jack?' There came a sigh.

'Don't you two ever stop? We just escaped loads of hairy orange men and the might of the London Underground and you're worried who was being chased the most!' Jack said exasperated.

'Well I'm certainly amazed at one thing,' Faiza said after a few moments' silence.

'What's that?' Wade muttered.

'That's the longest speech your friend has ever made!' They laughed in the darkness as the muffled sounds above them continued.

'Move on, nothing to see here.' Above the trio, Mr Tim and two men in Hi-Viz jackets were continuing to keep people moving and look all around them for where the 'troublemakers' could have gone. Mr Tim's radio crackled;

'Can't see nothing down here, Tim,' it said as Tim frowned. He pressed the talk button.

'This is Tim to all staff – we lost 'em. Keep your eyes peeled, they can't have vanished!' He looked suspiciously at the wall and kicked it lightly.

'Right, this is no good,' he said, still looking up and down the escalator. 'Let's see if we can find them again. Lorram, you wait here in case they come back this way. Colin, you come with me and we'll see what they did down on the platform.' Mr Tim and Colin left towards the Northern Line platform. Lorram stood determinedly with his back to the door and his arms crossed. A few people looked at him but carried on to their destinations.

From above them, the noise of people seemed to fade and settle to a faint background hum.

'We did it! Well, you did it – how did you get the tile to open then?' Wade asked. His voice seemed much louder now that it was quieter.

'I worked out what that code meant – you're right, it wasn't '2N4' but '2N1; the 1 was crossed out.'

'Which means?' cut in Faiza impatiently.

'Which must mean, socket 2 Not 1! I found that out the hard way; the first socket was a little bit live still!' Jack sighed.

'Glad you're ok. Glad we're ok,' Wade added.

'Yeah, that was definitely bad for you. You're too young to smoke!' Faiza replied. A nervous laughter trailed off as they realised they were stuck in a pitch-black room with no way out.

'Hang on.' From Faiza's direction came a very bright light. 'That's better – my phone has a built-in torch.' She shone it at the two boys who blinked furiously, before shining it on their surroundings. They were in a very small room – some might even call it a cupboard. The walls were plain brick and the back wall was just two metres away. The ceiling above them was dusty and grimy, with no trace of how they got in. Faiza moved the light and made out a red metal bucket, a very old looking broom, and a spade. Behind those was a poster. It was clearly very old, but in good condition – it had a picture of lots of people in smart old-fashioned dress with the words *Underground for business or pleasure* written across it.

'Oh, how are we going to get out of here?' Wade moaned. 'No-where to go, people waiting outside for us and, hey, can we phone for help?' In the darkness Jack shook his head, as Faiza checked her phone.

'No signal.' She frowned. 'Hey, look at this poster, it must be from like a hundred years ago!'

'1930s I'd say,' Jack said getting up and running his finger down the poster. 'Must be worth a lot, even if it is covered in dust.'

'So that socket released a catch that let the tile open, but it's reset and locked again now?' Wade asked.

'Yeah. Besides, we'd never get back up there to open it,' replied Jack tapping the wall.

'But why go to all that trouble to unlock the entrance to this place, if it's just a cupboard? Is the bucket made of gold?' Wade asked, as he kicked it noisily. 'Ow, no it's just iron.'

'So, we just wait here till they get that hatch open and arrest us?' asked Faiza.

'It'll be something good to say in Monday's creative writing session!' replied Wade. Jack ignored them and put his ear to the poster.

'There, yes, there, got it,' Jack said quietly. 'Can you shine the light here on the poster? They went quiet as Faiza lit the poster up. Jack had his finger in the middle of the poster, on what looked like a woman's glove. He pushed it gently, but nothing happened. He pushed a little harder and suddenly vanished.

'Jack?' asked Wade and he moved quickly towards where Jack had been, bumping into Faiza. They were suddenly plunged in darkness as Faiza's phone hit the floor with a splintering crunch.

'Oh no, my phone!' came Faiza's voice.

12

'Jack, Jack are you ok? Where are you?' Wade asked frantically. There were some coughing and scuffling noises.

'Yeah, I'm ok.' He stuck his head through a large hole. 'Climb through.' With Jack pulling, Wade climbed through.

'What about my phone?' Faiza hissed. She scrambled in the dark and picked up the remains of her phone.

'Whatever – just get through!' replied Wade.

'It'd better be safe the other side of that hole!' Faiza moaned.

'Might be a squeeze for you,' Wade said to Faiza once he was in.

'Shut it or I'll land on you!' She made it through and stood up slowly. With no light, all three of them walked about with their arms in front of them.

After a few seconds there was a scraping noise, followed by an exclamation.

'I found a chair!' It was Faiza. More noises; scraping and paper being moved followed by a glass smashing.

'Oops, I think I found a glass... well, bits of glass.' Wade laughed.

'Aha!' Jack said excitedly, 'I've got it'

'Where on earth is your little friend taking us?' laughed Faiza.

'His name is Jack. *Jack*,' Wade said defensively. Before Faiza had a chance to reply, the room was bathed in light. They looked up and saw that connected to a newly lit lamp was a long brown flex and connected to that was Jack.

'Surprised it still works. Where are we?' Jack said as they all looked around. The brick-lined musty room was about four metres long and three metres wide. Towards one end were some upturned chests littered with paper and surrounded by three spindly chairs, one of which was occupied by Faiza. Everywhere was covered in a thin layer of dust and the air was stale. The walls were bare except for some pieces of paper and ancient Underground posters. In one of the corners was a large, pale, wooden chest, with 'Indian Tea' stencilled on it. Some empty tins and scraps of paper were strewn around the place, as well as what looked like cables and an old-fashioned telephone.

Faiza was still looking sadly at her phone, before shoving it in her top pocket. 'It's broken – if we get out of here I'm making you pay for it.'

'Whatever,' replied Wade, nonchalantly running his finger along the wall. He walked towards Jack.

'Looks like a sort of storage room that people forgot when they built the place,' Wade said, examining some of the posters. Faiza found the telephone and followed the cable to under another large box. Smiling, she carefully pushed it out the way, only to find the cable just ended, like it had been pulled out from the wall somewhere.

A few metres above them, Mr Tim and Colin returned unhappily from the Northern line.

'They appeared yet, Lorram?' Mr Tim asked, trying the silver door again.

'Not yet, sir, I kept an eye on everyone passing, but nothing. What about you?' replied Lorram.

'We found where the kids were, but it just looks like a couple of old shorted-out sockets,' said Colin also trying the door. 'We reckon they were just mucking around – must have surprised 'em, that one being live!'

'Yeah, but where are the little bleeders now?' Mr Tim pushed the door again.

'Reckon they slipped out with some of the other passengers,' said Lorram.

'Damn,' said Mr Tim, 'probably long gone by now then.' Shrugging his shoulders, he stared down at the front of his boot. There was a small piece of paper stuck to the underneath. Carefully he picked it off and unfolded it. He squinted at a string of letters and numbers.

'What do we do now then?' asked Colin, who also tried the door. Mr Tim looked up from the piece of paper and stared at them both incredulously. He paused then said in a deadpan voice.

'We do this: One – we alert the Bank control room to get copies of their images to send to the Transport police and other main stations. Two – keep an eye on all the cameras and let me know if you see those *Herberts* again.' As Mr Tim reeled off their list of jobs, the other two men appeared to be making mental notes. 'Oh, and I want a news blackout on this. I know some of the public will be talking about it, but to the outside world it never happened, got it?' Colin and Lorram looked at each other, a little puzzled.

'Are they really that important, sir? They were just having a laugh and no real harm done,' stated Lorram. Mr Tim shook his head and jabbed his finger in Lorram's chest.

'Listen to me,' he replied. 'You see these kids, or your friends see these kids or the BTP see these kids, they tell me – no-one else but me, got it?'

'Yep, got it,' they mumbled in unison, a little puzzled.

'Right, off you go – Lorram, to the WC line, Colin; the DLR line and keep 'em peeled.' Mr Tim watched them go. He kicked the silver door once more, before heading up the escalators in a bad mood to the control room.

13

In the dim light, Wade bent down and rummaged in a wooden box. Through a cloud of dust, he produced a lamp with a thick stick nailed to the bottom of it. 'Why have these two lamps got sticks attached to them?'

'No idea – is there anything else there?' asked Jack, who was exploring the rest of the room.

'You know, for a moment I thought we might find some gold stacked up in here,' said Wade, as he looked around wistfully. Faiza went over to some paper on the floor where they had come through and opened her eyes wide.

'Hey,' she said slowly, 'look at this!' The boys came over to her. Faiza pointed at the newspaper. *'Berlin Bombs drive Hitler to frenzied attacks on Britain!'* The headline of the *Sunday Express* declared fearfully. Jack peered at the date – it said, *'Sunday 1st September 1940'*.

'Wow, that's a few days before the Blitz started. Was this just an old storeroom?' said Wade.

'Why would they have such a complicated entry? No, this place was used for something else,' Jack replied. 'Something that needed lamps on sticks and –' He stopped as he heard a rustling on the boxes behind him. One of the papers fluttered to the floor.

'Hey, maybe there's something in all those papers?' Wade nodded over at the top of the chests. All three of them walked over there as the light flickered. Most of the papers had faded scribbles on and some were blank, but underneath the papers was a large Underground map.

'Hey there's Bank station.' He handed it to Jack. Jack looked at it, then handed it to Faiza.

'Yes, and there's *Monument* and *King William Street* Station? I've not heard of that before. It says it's by *Monument* station between *Bank* and *London Bridge*.'

'That's where we walked just an hour ago – how can a station just disappear?' asked Wade.

'It must have been knocked down for some other building I guess,' pointed out Jack. 'Maybe the tunnels are still there?'

'Why is there an X at the bridge?' asked Faiza.

'And look, another one to the left of that *King William Street*!' pointed out Wade excitedly. 'This must be something to do with the gold going missing, it just must!'

'That *King William Street* station looks different to the rest of the map,' cut in Jack. 'It's just drawn in.' All three peered at the small oblong. It was situated at right angles to Monument station, at the far end of London bridge.

'So,' said Wade still excitedly, 'the gold train travelled through these stations, but disappeared under the bridge?'

'I don't remember reading that the gold train even went through Monument or that other station.' Jack scrunched his face up. Faiza didn't say anything but sat back looking bemused.

'What?' asked Wade. 'You're nearly smiling – it's scary.'

'You actually may be onto something here,' she said. 'If you are, I may forgive you that you broke my phone and got me covered in dust and dirt.'

'Ah you're always grubby. And I didn't break your

rubbish old phone – even Jack's great-great-grandad has got a phone newer than that brick!' Wade scoffed.

'When we get back and you're grounded for a year, this broken phone is all you'll have to remind you of the outside world!' she retorted. As Jack put the map and some of the other papers into his bag, the light began to flicker and unconsciously they all held their breath. After a few moments, it steadied.

'Oh, let's just get out of here,' Faiza said a little less surely.

'How can we get out if we can't open that hatch?' Wade asked.

'Maybe there's another way out?' replied Jack looking intently at the desk.

'I wouldn't bank on that – anyway we'll probably die in here and get eaten by small terrifying things that were once probably mice or rats,' she said, looking around nervously at the floor.

'But that hatch is airtight,' said Jack smiling, 'so no air can get in or out from there which is good.'

'Great, so the choices are being shot by London Underground for being idiots or terrorists, being eaten alive by rat-type black greasy things or suffocating, with Wade's stupid face being the last thing I see.'

'Hang on – Jack, why is that good if there's no air?' asked Wade.

'Wait a minute and see,' he replied with a knowing look. Faiza was about to tell them both what a waste of space they were, when they heard a distant rumble which faded as quickly as it had begun. A few seconds later, one of the papers on the desk rustled. They all looked intently at it. Jack smiled as a lightbulb appeared above both their heads.

'Where is the air coming from?' Wade blurted.

'I think the air is from a grate somewhere in here,' replied Jack. With a click of her fingers, Faiza remembered the crate she had moved earlier and went over to it. Pushing the crate even further along, she saw a white grate with holes in it. Holding her hand and then her ear to it, she could feel a gust of cool foul air.

'Here, here it is!' she shouted joyously and a sheet on the table rustled as the boys ran over. Jack opened his bag and got out the remnants of his dad's Spitfire. He pushed the remaining wing tip into the end of one of the painted screws and managed to unscrew it. Repeating it with the other screw, he was happy to hear the grate clatter to the floor.

'What's down this smelly hole?' Wade asked nervously; he wasn't even sure he was looking into a hole; it was so dark. He picked up something small and hard that was next to the hole – probably a piece of telephone – and threw it into the hole. All three of them held their breath as the object bounced off the sides in the darkness. A few seconds passed as the noise simply faded.

'Oh God,' said Faiza, the tension rising in her voice, 'if there's anything else alive in that tunnel, I'm making sure it gets you first, so off you go!'

'Well I'm not –' Wade started to say but didn't finish as he felt a shove from behind and he plummeted away. Behind him, Jack got into the hole a little more slowly, but rapidly gained speed.

'Oh,' sighed Faiza loudly, 'here we go again.' And with a scream, she too climbed into the hole and down into the abyss.

14

Faiza was sliding in the darkness; she couldn't tell whether her eyes were open or not. Although she started off slowly in the half-metre wide tunnel, she sped up in no time. All she could think about was that she would slide into some rat thing or worse: the bones of people that died in the tunnels. The smell was getting worse and as she dared to put one hand out, she felt the walls were slippery. Just what was lying in wait for her at the end? Faiza was just getting the confidence to stick her arms and legs out to try and slow down or stop when the world disappeared from beneath her.

For a moment Faiza flailed her arms and legs in the air, before landing with a jolt on top of something softer than the hard bricks she had just left. She tried to scream, but the sudden stop left her winded. She laid there for a moment before sitting up, breathing heavily. It wasn't completely dark now, and this larger tunnel seemed to be naturally lighter, as if lit from a luminescent glow.

Looking up, she noticed in the semi-darkness that both Wade and Jack were standing and laughing a few metres away. Slowly, and with a growing sense of dread, she looked down to see just what she had landed on. It filled her with revulsion – she was on a bed of white, sticky fat stuff. She reached out at it and pulled her now fat-en-crusted hand away quickly. She screamed and tried to stand up, but fell over again, which just made the boys laugh even more. She shouted at them as they reached out to grab her, pulling her onto the thin brick sill.

'Look at me! Just look at me!' She tried to brush the fat material off herself. Some of it did come off, but a lot of it seemed to just smear. 'Look at me!' she screamed again. The boys both doubled with laughter and Faiza shouted at them to shut up.

As the boys laughed, Faiza mumbled and patted herself down – it didn't seem to be removing any of the crud at all. Unexpectedly from above, a few large dollops of some dark material and liquid landed on and about Wade and Jack. The boys' laughing instantly turned to protestation. Looking up, Faiza could see the hole they had come down was next to other holes the same size all along this tunnel in both directions. She pushed herself against the wall in case more came from above. The boys frantically tried to remove some of the mess that now caked their clothes too.

'Thanks a lot and serves you right.' she sneered. 'Now it's you two that smell like a farmyard!'

'We're covered in some really smelly stuff here!' Wade complained.

'How come it was *me* that landed on the fat dump?' Faiza said, pointing at the mound in the middle of the small stream.

'You shot out of there like a cannonball!' exclaimed Wade. 'I sort of dribbled out and Jack landed on me in front of that pile of... well, Jack thinks it's leftover fat.'

'Does he. Good for him. Does he know how to get it out of my hair?' she screeched. Jack was about to reply, when she continued; 'Still it's better than that stuff that landed on you!' she laughed. Wade scrunched up his nose; whatever was on his head and clothes smelled very bad indeed.

'I did hurt my ankle a bit,' Wade said, rubbing his ankle, 'but Jack didn't, as I broke his fall.' He laughed a little, but no-one else did.

'Well, we don't need no Sherlock to work out that this is a sewer. A big fat smelly sewer,' said Faiza.

The tunnel itself was about three metres high, with a half metre brick sill along the left-hand edge. In the trickle of water were large lumps; possibly fat deposits, possibly something else. Behind them, the world seemed to vanish into the darkness. In front of them, the tunnel vanished around to the right, but was dotted either side and in the roof by black circles. Jack explained that they were the smaller sewers leading into this larger one. Faiza stopped and looked dubiously at the ceiling, before looking at Wade.

'You really ok?' she asked quietly. Wade looked back at her before looking down and rubbing his ankle.

'Yeah, I guess. You?' he asked.

'I'm ok. And – erm – you?' she looked at Jack, who just nodded. 'Wonder where we are… must be halfway to the Thames, eh?'

'Let's keep walking', said Wade peering forward.

'Well, I ain't crawling back up any tunnels!' stated Faiza her voice slightly echoing.

'We'd best follow this larger one; it's bound to lead to the river,' said Jack, indicating the stream flow.

'You can go first this time, Captain Quiet.' Carefully

they made their way along the side of the sewer. As they walked, they could hear what seemed like distant water-falls and Wade was certain that any second they would be swept away by another flood of who knew what? Water and other material poured or tickled out of many of the holes above and beside them.

'Jack, you did brilliantly – you got us out of there!' said Wade as they walked.

'Yeah and he also got us in there,' said Faiza curtly, but with a wry smile.

15

As they rounded the bend, they all gasped. There in the gloomy distance was a small speck of light. They sped up a little. Wade overtook Jack and a few minutes later came to a large iron grille. Through it he could see another brick wall, and to the right of it, he could just make out the river. The iron grille barring their way was very solid and rusty with gaps of around five centimetres between each bar.

'Oh that's just great – now what?' asked Wade, grabbing the bars in anger. 'Isn't it just the perfect end to a crap day, that we are going to be trapped here forever in sewer hell?' There was no reply. He looked around and to his horror, he found he was talking to himself. Faiza and Jack had vanished. 'Hello? Hello?' he shouted frantically. Silence.

'Up here, Squib!' The voice echoed around the cavernous brickwork, but it seemed to come from back inside the tunnel. It was Faiza.

'What, where?' he started.

'Small staircase with a gate to your left about ten metres back, you twonk. Come and join us, it's much fresher up here!' she said. He backtracked into the gloom and found the small gate.

The gloomy brick staircase wound around a central column and, after climbing twenty or so steps in the semi-darkness, he found Faiza and Jack.

'What's above?' asked Wade.

'No idea, but this door was hard to move even with me and your friend pushing it,' replied Faiza. 'Let's try it again, but with all of us.' They nodded and squeezed together in the cramped staircase. At first nothing happened, except for some creaking. They pushed again; shoulders pressed against the wood. Above them they heard some movement and then a crashing sound as the door eased open. They squeezed up through and past some metal posts and what looked like gardening equipment. The stairs they had come up on continued upwards, but they were looking at a small black door which was less than one and a half metres high. Faiza reached out to the brass knob. All three of them held their breath, as the door creaked open.

They emerged cautiously into the bright sunlight. The first thing that hit Wade was the fresh air! It was glorious, but also reminded him how awful they smelled. They were in a small church courtyard next to a busy main road. Wade looked back at the door they had come from; *Danger: Authorised personnel only* it said, in big letters on a scruffy piece of paper.

'Saint Magnus the Martyr,' Faiza read out from the plaque on the pillar. A loud clanging noise suddenly made them jump – the bells in the tower were being rung above them.

'That's where the steps go up to!' said Jack clicking his fingers. He listened intently for a moment. 'Beautiful mathematical patterns.' The other two just looked at him strangely.

'Come on, Colonel Clanger,' Faiza said, as they headed away from the church, along a pavement that led to the river. Less than a minute later, they came to a metre-high wall that bordered the river, listening to the peal of bells that seemed to echo everywhere.

'Let's stop there!' Wade pointed to some hoarding that was hiding some workmen's tools and works. Behind it, Faiza took her shoes off and gasped at the stench. Jack and Wade decided not to take theirs off.

'Ugh, I am going to smell like that place forever!' moaned Faiza.

'What's new?' laughed Wade, before realising he smelled just the same.

'Listen, let's go home, have a clean-up and work out what we've got and where we can go next,' said Faiza, shaking out some crud from her laces.

'Let's avoid Bank Station though eh?' Jack added. He put his hands in his jacket then ran them through his trouser pockets. 'Damn, I've lost the bit of paper with the code on.'

'So, we'll just print another one, but I don't think we need it anymore,' said Wade.

'Sure, it's just that I don't usually lose things.' Jack sighed, looking puzzled and annoyed.

'Do you think they'll be looking for us?' said Wade.

'Oh yeah, you bet.' Faiza frowned, as she put one of her feet in her soggy trainers.

'I know – we can follow the Thames path to Embankment,' said Jack looking behind the hoardings at a sign, 'and get the tube from there.' They put on their still-wet outer clothes and got up. Carefully, and checking there was no-one observing them, they made their way from behind the hoarding and back onto the path.

'Sorry about your phone,' said Wade quietly. She frowned and picked it from her top pocket. It was still dead.

'Ah well, I was going to give it to you for your birthday anyway,' she replied.

'Could just use it as a doorstop.' He laughed.

'No-one is ever going to believe this you know,' said Jack; his shoes making a squeaking noise.

'Well, no-one is going to find out, are they?' replied Faiza. 'At least not until we've worked it all out and found some gold or a reward!'

'We can't tell our parents, they'll just ground us forever and make us say sorry to Mr Tim or something else unfair,' replied Wade.

'I can imagine him at the station, still looking for us!' giggled Faiza. They all laughed.

'I said I'd be at my dad's shop after lunch, so we'd better hurry. Wow, I'm whiffy!' said Jack, squelching in his shoes.

'What's new?' replied Wade, smiling. 'Just keep your head down.' If they had have looked up and behind them, they would have seen a large building with dark windows. If they had looked even closer, they would have seen one of the CCTV cameras pointed right at them.

16

The smelly trio kept their heads down and got on the Northern line at Embankment. They ignored the faces of other passengers, many of whom scrunched their faces up but were too polite to say anything.

Jack got up to leave at Oval. 'I hope my dad doesn't say anything about my clothes.' He headed off the train and up the stairs. Wade and Faiza continued to sit in pongy silence, until they arrived at Stockwell a few minutes later.

'If I can't get this stuff out of my hair, I'm going to be seriously unhappy,' said Faiza as they walked back.

'I don't think anyone would notice,' replied Wade, deadpan.

'So says *Mr Fashionable* – at least my clothes are this century and look like they were made for someone my size,' sneered Faiza.

'And what a size that is!' said Wade, as he raced ahead.

'Just you wait, Squib!' she shouted after him. A few minutes later, she let herself into the flat. Wade was in the shower already, so she went to her room and changed into her dressing gown. Both of them were pleased there was still no-one in.

Wade put on fresh clothes and hoped no-one would ask why his other clothes were so smelly and dirty. Just then Faiza tapped on Wade's door, and he opened it.

'We'll tell Mum & your dad we have to go back tomorrow for some other reason.'

'Yeah, I reckon we should start at London Bridge,' Wade replied smiling.

'Great – and then we can get some answers. Your friend has got all the papers, hasn't he?'

'Jack, yeah. He'll be over later, and we can figure it all out! Hey, we did good, eh?' said Wade. Faiza paused and just nodded.

Two and a half hours later and Wade's room looked very much like it had the previous day; sheets of paper littering the floor and in the middle of it sat an excited Wade. The door creaked open and in walked Jack.

'Guess what, I know what the dotted lines mean!' Jack enthused.

'Ah great, mate!' replied Wade, trying to move some of the papers so his friend could sit down. Jack produced the old map excitedly.

'Where's your sister?'

'Faiza? Think she went out to get some hair gel,' he replied nonchalantly.

'Well, hopefully we all smell a little better than we did earlier!' Jack said with a smirk. 'I spoke to my great-great-grandad – Albert – and we worked out what the lines mean!' He looked excited. Wade just looked at him expectantly.

'Well?' he finally spluttered.

'Ah, glad you asked,' he replied, grinning, 'Look – when they started building the Underground, they built these tunnels, then after a while they found they were too small or they needed bigger trains. So, they built new tunnels and blocked up the old ones. There's quite a few of them apparently.'

'So these dotted lines are what, the old tunnels that ran to London Bridge? So down there under where we were, are some empty abandoned tunnels?' Wade was fascinated.

'Yes, and no,' replied Jack. 'My great-great-grandad remembers that there *did* used to be an old disused station called *King William Street* at one end of London Bridge, but he's sure the tunnels went under that road.' He pointed to Arthur Street, which was inlaid with the two dotted lines. 'He remembers it 'cos his brother was called Arthur.'

'Wow, do you reckon the tunnels still exist? Wouldn't it be fabulous if the gold was still down there somehow, just sitting there waiting to be discovered?' Wade had a far-away look in his eyes. He saw himself opening a disused door, heading down some stairs and finding something shiny and amazing!

'Apparently, when the war started, they opened up one of the tunnels to shelter from the Blitz.' Wade grabbed the paper and spread it out, looking intently at the dotted lines. He pointed to the north end of London Bridge.

'Well we HAVE to go and look at that place – can't believe we walked near there earlier today!' Wade said.

'Yeah,' replied Jack. 'I guess if the tunnels still exist, there must be a way in from the surface – a secret way!'

'Yeah, great idea. I hope it's that easy!' Jack said. 'Well, we had better let your sister know,' he added. Wade's smile faded a little.

'Oh, I'm not sure,' Wade said glumly.

'Come on, she's pretty good in a tight spot and she has helped,' said Jack.

'Are you sure you're not just scared of her?' teased

Wade. 'Or do you fancy her?' Jack grabbed a pillow and hurled it at Wade, who dodged it, laughing.

Jack was about to throw the other one, when the door opened and in walked Faiza. Her hair was standing on end, but this time by design. Jack and Wade stopped.

'Hey, it's Captain Quiet and the Sewer King!' she exclaimed.

'Well, either you got scared or you got your hair gel!' quipped Wade. Faiza just looked at him.

'Hilarious,' she replied, raising an eyebrow. 'At least I have real hair rather than a reject mop. Anyway, I feel much fresher now. Hey, on the way back I stopped at the library.'

'I'm amazed – I didn't know you could read!' said Wade, nudging Jack.

'Can read better than you. Anyway look, I found out some stuff. There's a whole section on the war, so I photocopied some of it.' She emptied her carry-bag of papers and books onto the bed.

'So, come on, what have you found out,' she asked. Wade just looked at Jack as she continued; 'Don't you try and leave me out of this, Squib – I'm in this as much as you.' Wade's features softened.

'Leave you out?' he protested. 'Never – I was actually just telling Jack we should definitely include you.' He beamed at her, which seemed to make her even more suspicious.

17

Ten minutes later and the three of them were sitting surrounded, or possibly swamped, by all the outpourings from their investigation. Each one of them was looking at a different piece of paper; Faiza a picture of a train, Wade; a police report and Jack had a grey, grainy picture. He passed it to Wade. It was of an unhappy-looking man with a thin-lipped grimace in a long expensive looking coat.

'So that's Horatio Plum?' asked Wade. 'Yeah, he looks guilty – he definitely did it.'

'Says here he worked in military intelligence in World War One and in the years afterwards. Came up with some ingenious code-breaking algorithms apparently,' said Jack, with almost a hint of admiration.

'He looks a bit shifty,' said Faiza nonchalantly. 'So what working theories have you and Billy Boffin come up with then?'

'We decided that Plum did it.' Wade recalled that one of their theories was that the gold was actually painted cake that the guards all ate, but he didn't need to share that with her. Faiza nodded and passed him a picture of a sinister-looking set of carriages.

'This is the actual train then? What kind was it?' asked Wade.

'According to this, the train was modified 1930s rolling stock. Look at it – it looks like a tank on wheels!' he exclaimed.

The black and white picture showed a two-carriage train which, even though it was grey, looked like all the colour had been removed *before* the picture was taken. The carriage closest to them was made from solid iron with lines of rivets littering the outside. There was one small horizontal slit just under where the curved roof joined the main body of the carriage. Through the slit, which the flash had lit up, something that looked like a sinister pair of eyes shone out – presumably one of the guards. The next carriage along was even darker and looked like the first one, but there were no slits, just a line with several strips of dark metal and large padlocks.

'Is that second one the one with the gold?' asked Wade. Jack nodded. At the front of the train was the engine. From what they could make out, it looked like a standard small steam engine, also painted black with *25209* in gold letters. From the angle where the picture was taken, there was a small hole through which they could see the shadow of a head. A dark arm protruded from the open cab.

'This picture goes with those ones.' Faiza thrust another picture in front of them. It showed the same train from the other angle, with the train driver in the front. The train driver was standing with his arm overhanging the edge of the cab and was clearly scowling. Behind him was a small circular window, a shovel with some coal and a cap hanging up. There was a shadow behind the driver.

'The driver would have to be in on it and maybe even some others too,' Jack said quietly, 'and I'm sure there's someone in the shadows of that cab.'

'But how could the gold have disappeared anyway? It would have taken loads of people to carry all that gold off,' said Wade looking at the pictures more intently.

'Says here,' replied Faiza, 'that the guards saw and heard nothing except it was a bit bumpy. So, what happened to the driver after the *incident*?' she asked, convinced they were onto something major now. Both Jack and Wade scrambled around looking for the paper that had some of the biographies. Wade snatched one up and read it out.

'The driver, *Jeff Damson*, was interviewed at length, along with all the soldiers and all were cleared. Maintained innocence blah blah driver blah blah.' Wade skipped through a lot of it. 'Ah, here we are, the final case notes from Corner say: 'He left his job three months later and stayed unemployed till his death.'

'And this gold-train driver just decided to leave his job one day and then die?' asked Faiza disbelievingly.

'Yes, sort of – says here that he was interviewed again in '43. He was just a tramp then apparently. They tried to find him in '47, before the case was closed, but he had died a few years earlier,' said Wade, scan-reading.

'How did he die?' Faiza asked, trying to take the paper off Wade.

'Found dead one night on the north bank of the Thames. *Natural causes* it says here, fuelled by years of drink and neglect.'

'Maybe then,' said Jack excitedly, 'only Plum knew where the gold was, and Damson never got his share!'

'Yes! Right, what did they find after the train turned up gold-less?' Faiza was excited now.

'They searched the tunnels but found nothing!' Jack said the last word with spooky emphasis.

'Nothing?' repeated Faiza.

'Well, nothing apart from a pair of bolt cutters and four ticket stubs for a train to Southampton,' replied Jack.

'That's like they were taunting anyone that came looking for them.' Said Wade.

'...Or they were trying to throw people off the scent,' said Jack thoughtfully.

'It all points towards the boss of the ministry. Could they have turned the gold into tracks?' asked Wade frowning.

'Gold rails? Seriously? But how *did* they get all that gold off the train?' Faiza said. 'It must have gone somewhere!'

'Maybe they just didn't find it because it's dark in the tunnels!' Wade laughed. No-one else did.

Wade quietly picked up the picture of Plum again and looked at it more closely. He leaned over to his chest of drawers and pulled a magnifying glass from the top. 'That ring's a bit odd, isn't it?' All three of them leaned in again and stared at the man's hand. On the first finger of his left hand was a small silver ring, the topmost part was black with a backwards C motif. The others shrugged their shoulders.

'Just a ring then I guess. So now what?' he said. Faiza looked him right in the eyes, and with a twinkle in hers said;

'First, I reckon we go and find that *King William Street* Station... or at least the remains of it, and maybe even the tunnels!'

18

Faiza hopped onto the platform at London Bridge from the train and looked around a little furtively as Wade and Jack joined her. They sat down on one of the benches that stretched along the platform, as the doors closed and the train sped out of the station in a gust of warm air.

'Don't see why we can't just get out at Bank,' moaned Wade as they headed up the escalator to the surface.

'Just in case *our friends* are still looking out for us,' explained Faiza, 'they might even be looking for us here!'

'Oh, come on!' replied Wade incredulously.

'Just remember, I've told Mum and Dad that we are going out to the Transport Museum, so I'm responsible for you – don't do anything daft,' instructed Faiza.

'Does that include being with you?' asked Wade. Faiza just shook her head.

Wade was aware of the TFL staff in bright orange and pink Hi-Viz jackets – were they looking at them? Why was one of them speaking furtively into the radio? Keeping their heads down, they headed through the gates and out of the station, stopping to cross the road near a small café. At the far end of the crossing stood a young man and his girlfriend, and next to them was a man in an unfashionable blue suit. This man seemed to be staring right at them, but then looked away at the traffic signal. Jack angled his head that way and nudged Wade who also saw him. He whispered to Faiza, and they all looked at the man before looking away. The traffic stopped and they began to walk across the road. The man in the blue suit started towards them.

They reached the middle of the road at the same time. To their amazement and relief, the blue-suited man strode right between Wade and Jack and simply continued. Wade and Faiza breathed a sigh of relief and, passing the couple, reached the other side of the road. Jack however remained anxious.

'Did you see that?' he said quietly.

'Yeah, look at us getting all worried over nothing!' laughed Wade, as they headed past the bus stop.

'Did you see what he had in his right ear?' he continued. They stopped and looked at Jack curiously. 'A wire! He had a wire.'

'Like they do on the news?' asked Wade.

'Like spies and heavies have,' Jack uttered. They all looked behind them, but there was no trace of the man.

'Really? Are you sure?' said Faiza unsurely, 'Maybe he was deaf and it was a hearing aid?' Faiza and Wade seemed happier now. 'Yeah, or he could have just been listening to classical music – he looked the type,' continued Faiza.

'He was just an ordinary bloke, you worry wart,' said Wade. 'Come on, let's get over the bridge!' Jack stayed quiet and bit his lip as he walked.

Heading away from the crossing, they walked across London Bridge. Wade stopped half-way across.

'Hey look, that's where we were yesterday!' he exclaimed,

pointing at the north bank where they had rinsed out their shoes and clothes. Jack stopped and bent to tie up his laces. Looking up, he saw a couple – a man and a woman – walking their way. Nothing special about that, but where had he seen them before? They seemed to be sharing a joke, and then stopped and looked out over the Thames, pointing out the Tower of London and other familiar tourist destinations. Jack breathed out slowly and moved quickly to join the others.

They walked along the bridge and over the foreshore, passing over Lower Thames Street. Faiza was a few steps in front of them, looking up at the building names.

'You alright, Jack?' Wade said looking oddly at Jack.

'Yeah, just a bit –' he replied.

'We'll be alright, mate. Come on, take your mind off things – let's find what we came here for,' said Wade quietly. 'Hey there's that church we were at yesterday – Saint Martyn the Magnificent or something?'

'What are you, our guide?' quipped Faiza. They came to a stop a few minutes later at the edge of the pavement. Behind them stood the white and gold Monument, a testament marking the Great Fire of London.

'Did you know,' said Jack, 'that it's sixty-one metres high and sixty-one metres from the start of the fire in Pudding Lane?' Wade and Faiza just looked at him.

'Well, I know the fire started in 1666, a year after the plague!' chipped in Wade, proud that he could add to the conversation.

'Why is it my lot in life to be surrounded by geeks and tour guides?' sighed Faiza. 'Right, geek squad, that map seemed to indicate it was right here on the edge of this road, by the *sixty-one-metre* monument,' she said, sarcastically emphasising the word sixty-one.

19

On the side of a building they found a blue plaque indicating this was the site of King William Street Underground station in 1890.

'The tunnels apparently went from about here and curved around to the river along Arthur Street.' He indicated across the road, where there were a lot of building works and hoardings along the length. They crossed the road and walked slowly down the pavement to the side of the street. Again, there was nothing to indicate that a few metres below their feet could be two ancient tube tunnels.

'Maybe we could go into the half-demolished building and see what's there?' enthused Wade. Jack and Faiza shook their head.

'That must be the most stupid idea I've ever heard, even for you, Squib,' Faiza said incredulously.

'Oh what do you know, Spikey?' retorted Wade, joining them on the bench. 'Have you got any better ideas?' He sighed and looked around half-hoping to see a sign saying, 'Route to the gold this way'.

They spent another ten minutes looking around the area; trying the handles of large foreboding doors and peering innocently behind hoardings. There was nothing to be found, and definitely not a sign saying, '*Hidden gold over here*'. Heading through the blue mosaic underpass, they climbed the stairs and stood on the pavement looking back down the bridge.

'That's it then,' said Wade dejectedly.

'Not quite. There is one more thing we can try,' replied Jack, frowning. Wade's eyes lit up.

'Your eyes won't light up quite as much when you realise what we'll have to do,' Jack replied solemnly. There was a pause as Jack's words soaked in.

'No way, uh uh,' cut in Faiza, before Jack had a chance to continue. Wade's smile changed to a frown before he nodded understandingly.

'OK. Let's do it. We have to,' Wade agreed.

'I told you I'm not doing it – you know how long it took to get that crap out of my hair and toes and –' Faiza was adamant.

'Ugh, look if it's our only way back in, we have to try it,' said Wade, ignoring her. 'That's what you meant isn't it, Jack?'

'I'm afraid so.' He looked towards the churchyard. 'If all three of us head back in, we might be able to find a way to one of the old King William Street tunnels.'

'But, really?' replied Faiza, a little less cross and a little more depressed. She looked around for inspiration, but found none.

Walking through the archway from Lower Thames Street, they stood again in the churchyard of Saint Magnus the Martyr. It seemed very quiet considering it was next to a busy road. Ominously quiet.

'Go on then, off you go.' Faiza stood with her hands in her pockets.

'Seriously? Me and Jack head down there and you just wait here?' moaned Wade. Faiza nodded.

'Seems fair to me,' she replied. 'You both go down, get covered in – erm – muck, find a way in that probably doesn't exist and then come back and let me know.'

'Well if we find it, we're not going to tell you!' said Wade.

'The only thing you'll find is more of that stuff!' She laughed.

'Come on Jack.' Wade began to walk away. 'And what are you going to do up here?'

'Keep guard,' she replied smugly.

'Guard us from what?'

'ME,' came a voice from behind the pillar to their left.

20

There stood a man in a blue suit. *That* man. In *that* blue suit. For a moment, there was stunned silence and then everything seemed to happen at once. A dozen people in dark vests and sunglasses came from everywhere and from nowhere, the church doors, the trees, the low walls, the bushes and from around corners. Jack recognised at least two of them – that apparently nice-looking couple. There was a lot of running and threatening and shouting and orders to, 'Get on the ground, lie on the ground now!'

The startled three needed no second telling; they immediately laid face down on the ground with their hands outstretched. The man in the blue suit stood over them and ensured their hands were bound tight with cable ties. There was some radio crackle and Wade heard a few words; 'secure' and 'locked down'. There was a scuffle of feet around them and suddenly it seemed a lot quieter.

After a few moments, and with a sharp nod of his head, he signalled to the two people nearest who hauled them to their feet.

'Who are you, what do you want?' screamed Faiza,

with more than a hint of panic. The man put a finger to Faiza's lips.

'You can either be quiet or I'll end your power to speak forever.' The man spoke slowly and deliberately. After a few seconds, he removed his finger. She remained wide-eyed as the men put blindfolds on each of them. The man pulled their restraints a little tighter and the two men marched them forcibly round the side of the church towards the path at the river's edge.

'Please,' pleaded Wade, 'don't hurt us, we were just –'

'One more word from you and I'll throw you and your little girlfriends in the river,' the blue-suited man hissed.

Although they couldn't see, they could tell they were being taken away from the river and down steps into somewhere enclosed. Jack was pushed down the last few stairs and he would have fallen over if he hadn't bumped against Wade. Some doors hissed open and the floor changed from hard to soft. The sounds diminished as well, almost as though the place they were in was heavily carpeted or soundproofed.

They were shepherded into what was probably a lift and Jack thought he could sense that the two people had left. There were a few electronic sounds and it felt like they were travelling upwards, or was it down? The doors hissed again, and they were led out along a soft floor. Faiza heard someone pressing four buttons on a keypad, followed by a loud clicking and they were pushed semi-stumbling into a room and were encouraged to sit down on some chairs. The footsteps faded and they sat there not knowing what to do next or what would happen.

Days passed, or maybe it was just seconds. Someone shuffled in their seat.

'Way?' Faiza whispered. No reply. 'Wade?' There came a rustling of clothing.

'Faiza?' came the eventual reply. 'You there?'

'Of course I'm here, who do you think called your name?' she replied curtly. Wade sighed; it was good to know she was ok.

'Jack? Jack, you there?' Wade whispered. 'Is Jack here?'

'I'm here. Where are we?' Jack asked. 'Can you see anything?'

'No and I can't move my hands from behind my –' he stopped mid-sentence as they heard four keys being punched and the door open.

'Who are you? Where are we? I demand you release us!' Faiza said loudly and with more confidence than she was feeling.

'Calm yourself. Just sit still and we'll get those restraints and blindfolds off you.' The voice was calm and northern Irish. Faiza heard a clicking and then felt someone approach her. Suddenly the blindfold disappeared, and the world became very light. She blinked a few times and, once her eyes adjusted, she saw Jack and Wade sitting close to her with their blindfolds removed too.

The room was quite large and bare, with light pastel colours. The blandness of the wall was only interrupted by a keypad next to the door. There was a long dark-grey table in front of them and on the other side was a silver laptop stencilled with 'CO8-4'. Behind that was the Irish-sounding woman. She was older than she sounded, Wade thought, as his wrist restraints were cut by someone behind him. He rubbed his wrists – they didn't particularly hurt; he had just seen people doing that in films.

The man in the blue suit came back round from behind them and sat down next to the woman, who had a blank expression. The three looked fiercely at him. He stared blankly back at them, although there did seem to be a trace of a smug smile.

'Right, you three, where shall we begin?' the woman said slowly, looking at some papers and files in front of her. No-one said anything for a moment, before Faiza spoke;

'What the hell do you think you're doing? Kidnapping us and –' The woman raised her hand and Faiza stopped.

'Please calm down or I'll have to separate and silence you.' She let the words hang in the air for a moment before continuing. 'First let me tell you, things are looking very bad for you three indeed. It says here that you three are guilty of the following offences: One; trying to start an electrical fire at Bank Station yesterday. Two; collaborating to cause injury on the London Underground possibly through terrorist activities. Three; trying to evade and hinder a TFL official in his official duties and four; basically being a pain in the rear end. What do you have to say for yourself?' She tapped the table with her pen, as if to emphasise a point.

'I'll tell you what I have to say for myself!' replied Faiza fiercely. 'We'll start with you explaining where you get off roughing us up and threatening us!'

21

The woman behind the laptop opened her eyes wider. She paused and looked them up and down, looking back to the file she had in front of her.

'Hang on, hang on. Who roughed you up and threatened you – not my agents surely? Which ones – I want to know,' she asked in a soft voice.

All three of them looked at the man in the blue suit and said loudly, 'He did!' He seemed a little taken aback and shook his head lightly. Her tone changed and the smile disappeared.

'Tell me what happened.'

'That git –' Faiza pointed right at Mr Blue-suit '– threw us to the ground, threatened to throw us in the river and said he would end my power to speak forever with his fingers on my face!'

'And he made sure our wrists were tied too tight!' added Wade.

'And he pushed me down the stairs,' added Jack quietly. The features on the lady's face darkened. She went very close to Mr Blue-suit's face and looked him right in the eye.

'Is this true?' she asked, almost too politely. Mr Blue-suit looked at her and then at the three and back at her. He seemed to be withering under her gaze.

'Well, I suppose yes, but they were dangerous and –' he replied. Suddenly she shot out a hand and held up one finger directly in front of his left eye. He froze.

'Apologise to them,' she said quietly. He genuinely looked fearful.

'Ahem, I'm – erm – sorry,' he said quietly. She looked back at the three sitting there spellbound and then back to him, before placing her hand back on the table.

'We have spoken about this before,' she said to him. Her voice was very quiet again now, but there was still steel in it, 'and I am giving you no more warnings. If this happens again, you'll find things very difficult. Do I make myself clear, Mister?' He nodded quickly. She put that smile back on her face and turned back to face them. All three looked at her with newfound respect.

'I'm so sorry you didn't have a nice journey here. We had to get you here and didn't know what kind of people you were, but there was no need for it to be nasty. Now let's start again. Tell me who you are.' The three shuffled uncomfortably in their seats and looked at each other. It was Faiza who spoke first again;

'Well, I was taught not to speak to strangers, so why don't you tell us who you are first.' She folded her arms and the woman sat back in her chair. She raised her eyebrows and nodded slowly.

'Very well. I'm a patient person and I would like you to know who it is you're dealing with… or not as the case may be.' She leaned forward again.

'I'm Miss Corner, Chief of Operations, and this, as you know, is my assistant Mr –'

'Ma'am,' the man in the blue suit cut in, 'we should not be telling them anything about us, they could be…' He stopped, as she waved a dismissive hand.

'I think we'll be ok,' she said slowly, as if talking to a

small child. 'They don't exactly look like terrorists – they look like kids.' She turned back to Faiza. 'We are CO8 – Covert Operations – and you're in one of our *Discussion Suites*. Now,' she said coolly, 'tell me something about you.'

'We are just kids,' blurted out Wade, 'and we were just mucking around. We didn't start a fire or hurt anyone, we were just –'

'Having a laugh that got out of hand,' continued Faiza. 'You can see we're not terrorists and we don't have an agenda or anything.'

'Hmm, I've come to much the same conclusion in just the last few minutes, you're hardly battle-weary fanatics. However, I do need you to explain a few things.'

The three sat there feeling uncomfortable. 'Just who are you? You appear to be the only young people in the world with no mobile devices on you. No phones, no ID. Just three *Oyster Zip* cards that say you came from Stockwell this morning and yesterday morning too.'

'You can tell that?' said Faiza blinking. 'Hmm, no point lying then.'

'There was never any point lying, young lady,' replied Miss Corner curtly.

'Well my phone broke yesterday – at the tube station actually – and he lost his at the War Museum, and he hasn't got one,' said Faiza, indicating Wade and Jack. The woman in charge continued to stare at them, as though that alone would make them confess to a crime.

'And so, again, the million-dollar question; who the hell are you all?' She sat back with an air of expectation.

'Oh, erm, I'm William Picard, and this is my friend Miles Sisko and that's his sister, Tasha Janeway,' Wade lied. Miss Corner nodded sagely.

'Well, that's good to see I'm in such good company – I'm James T. Kirk by the way.' Miss Corner's voice dropped an octave. 'Shall we tell the truth my geek friend, rather than pretend we are Star Trek characters?' Jack was impressed judging by the look on his face. Faiza poked Wade and tutted. After a few seconds, she spoke;

'OK, ok. I'm Nataskie Smith, this is my brother Kashive and his friend Zac. That's the truth. Sorry about those trekkie names,' Faiza said shaking her head. Miss Corner stared at Wade, who just smiled meekly and looked down.

'That's *Trekker* names,' Jack corrected her, then went quiet as Faiza stared at him.

'That's better. Now, why were you down the Underground – twice?' Miss Corner asked, writing down some of the details. The man just continued to stare right at them.

'We were just going to visit – we went to the War Museum and they said there are loads of places that were used as refuges in the Blitz,' said Wade excitedly.

'Yes, and I had to go with them as I'm the oldest,' continued Faiza.

'See, the truth wasn't too difficult, was it?' Miss Corner agreed.

'So, what is this report about you trying to start an explosion in the station?' She looked directly at Jack. He squirmed a little and was about to speak when Wade spoke.

'That's just nonsense! We were looking at a plug socket that was sparking and when we went to report it, that Mr Tim bloke tried to blame us and chased us around the station!'

'So why did you run away when you were ordered to stop and how did you eventually get out of the station without being seen by anyone?' she asked. Wade was about to speak when this time Faiza cut in.

'Ah, just lucky I guess. The man – Mr Tim something or other – seemed mighty angry and hell-bent on making us pay, so we thought we'd better just get out of there.' The others nodded as Faiza continued, 'We walked out the main exit and no-one stopped us. You must have seen us on the CCTV?' said Faiza. Miss Corner looked at the blue-suited man, who briefly shook his head and continued staring at the three.

22

'Another question – how did you end up by the riverbank covered in – erm – muck without appearing on any other CCTV at all, either at Bank or any of the seventeen cameras leading to that area?' She turned the laptop round and they watched amazed. On the right of the screen they could see themselves the day before, walking down the path next to the church, climbing behind the hoarding and sitting on the Thames path.

'Just lucky I guess; look – we were just having a laugh. Just out of shot of your camera, we went down on the actual riverbank. I know we're not supposed to go down there, but it was a hot day!' said Faiza laughing.

'We've learned our lesson, so please don't tell my mum; we'll all be grounded for life!' continued Wade. Miss Corner leaned forward in her chair, scanning their faces.

'And why were you back at our glorious church *Saint Magnus the Martyr* this morning then?' she asked more intently. 'More jolly japes on the Underground or some other less-nice reason?'

'Well look, as you can see, we didn't get very far yesterday so we came back today to do more research,' volunteered Wade. 'Isn't that right, Zac?' Jack stayed quiet but looked pensive.

'In the churchyard? Why there?' she asked.

'It was bombed in the war, and we wanted to see if there was any bomb damage. As you saw, we passed it yesterday,' Faiza said. Miss Corner cocked her head slightly to one side. She wasn't sure if she believed them and yet it all sounded so plausible; there was something they weren't telling her. Jack put his hand up. Miss Corner smiled.

'You don't need to put your hand up. Are you going to say much the same thing?'

'Why would a secret surveillance and operations department be interested in a relatively minor disturbance at a tube station?' Jack asked. Miss Corner raised her eyebrows and nodded.

'You know, Zac, that's an excellent question. Clearly, you're all very well educated, and we can't pull the wool over your eyes. Truth is, my associate passed this file to me yesterday afternoon and he said they had had a tipoff that you three were prime suspects in a possible terrorist threat. Then when I came in this morning, I was informed you'd been identified at London Bridge again, so we arranged to follow you and then pick you three up. And here you all are. But are you youngsters really a terrorist threat?' There was a long pause.

'I don't think so,' she said eventually. The man next to her cleared his throat loudly and Miss Corner looked right at him. 'You have a problem?'

'It's just that these, these "wannabe anti-social behaviour order youths", have been causing trouble and mayhem on a big scale, as well as being a danger to themselves and others. I think we should be prosecuting them and setting an example to other would-be troublemakers,' he said with malice, sitting back and folding his arms.

'I appreciate your comments, Mister but look at them. They're just teenagers who made a few wrong decisions

and got caught out. We'll let them go.' On that last sylla-
ble, she stared at her assistant.

For a second it seemed like there would be defiance, but
after a few moments, Mr Blue lowered his eyes. She turned
back to face them.

'I'm sorry you were caught up in this, but please, please be
careful,' she said, looking them right in the eyes now, 'and
steer clear of tube stations. Now we need a few more details.'

'Miss Corner?' asked Jack suddenly, 'Did you have
anyone in your family who was also in security services?'
She stopped and looked at him with a look of bemusement.

'Why, yes. But what's that got to do with anything?
What do you think you know?' Her manner had changed.
Jack squirmed a little and replied;

'Oh nothing, it's just that, as my friend said, we're
studying London in the war and I thought I heard that
name mentioned somewhere.' Miss Corner narrowed her
eyes and looked him up and down.

'Hmm. Well I guess you might have heard my surname
then I suppose. My grandfather worked for the secret service in the war. The reason you might have heard of him
is because –' Her voice trailed off. She appeared to be pondering something and then she appeared to look like she
had solved something.

'That's it, isn't it?' She stared at each of them in turn.
'You've heard the story of *Corner's Calamity* and you want
to find the hidden gold. Well, let me tell you you're wast-
ing your time.'

'Corner's what? What gold? There's gold?' Wade said,
using the same kind of enthusiasm he had used when
he thought there really was gold. 'I mean, I heard a train
went missing with some gold somewhere, but I had no
idea it was still around!'

'You never told me there was gold!' Faiza poked Wade, who recoiled rubbing his arm. Miss Corner put her hands up.

'Are you three really saying that you're not after some mythical wartime gold? That you're not following some idea of getting yourselves killed by hunting around dangerous live tube tunnels for something that doesn't exist?' She pointed her pen at them in a semi-threatening way.

'Of course not! We were just looking at the history of the tube in World War Two!' Said Wade, almost convincing himself and wishing he was at home now.

'Because if you were,' Miss Corner continued, 'I'd tell you to just run home and find something else to occupy your time. It's not called *Corner's Calamity* for nothing.' The man in the blue suit looked at her with a slightly strange look in his eye as she continued. 'My grandad William, Inspector Corner, spent years on it... investigated hundreds of criminals and spent so many man-hours on it. It kind of broke him. He died over thirty years ago now, convinced he was so close.' Miss Corner continued to stare at them – didn't she ever blink?

'Right anyway, I need to go. Just promise me you'll keep out of tunnels and remember not to believe tales of missing gold – forget I said anything about it.' She handed Faiza a small white card. 'Use that card if you do see anything suspicious. My associate will take your details – the real ones – and then see you out. My advice is to keep clear of tube stations and don't do any more research on the ground, or under it.' Jack craned his neck slightly at her, as though his collar was too tight. After keying in the four-digit number, Miss Corner pulled the door and was gone.

23

The silence in the room seemed louder than ever. After a few moments, the man in the blue suit stood up slowly and walked around behind the trio. He put his face next to Faiza and said quietly in her ear.

'No-one knows you're here but me now. I might just take you to the basement and leave you there in the dark for a few days. If you do ever get out of here, you'll need to look over your shoulder and, when you do, I'll be there. I'm going to make your life hell…' He put his hand gently on her head.

Suddenly Faiza jammed her elbow backwards at considerable speed. Everyone in the room heard a loud exhalation of air, followed by a crack and something large and heavy smacking the table and then hitting the floor. All three of them stood up, ready for the noise and kerfuffle that was bound to follow, but he lay there face-up, with a spot of blood on his forehead and what looked like a large red mark.

'Wow, go sis!' said Wade, mouth agape. Faiza approached the man and moved his arm lightly with her foot. He made a faint groaning noise.

'Well, at least he's alive,' said Jack quietly.

'Shame. We have to get out of here now!' Faiza shouted. She tugged at the door, but it wouldn't budge. 'Damn, what's the code?'

'Jack, your turn!' Wade shouted and Jack ran over to the keypad. He closed his eyes and pressed the same four digits he had seen Miss Corner enter.

After a long, long second, there was a click and Faiza pulled the door. It opened and she looked up and down the corridor, before signalling to the others that it was clear. The corridor was carpeted and there were several doors off to left and right, each marked by a keypad. The place was soundless – maybe spies didn't work at the weekend. Hugging the walls and fearing they would be found out any second, they reached the end of the corridor. The number next to the panel said '4'. Wade repeatedly pressed the button to summon the lift.

'Don't use the lift, the heavies are always in the lift!' said Jack, pointing at the door to his left that was unsurprisingly marked 'stairs'. Faiza tapped him on the head and they sped into the stairwell. Wade looked over the bars at the top and almost wished he hadn't. Although they were only on the fourth floor, the stairwell seemed to go down and down forever.

'It's clear, let's go!' Wade's voice echoed for several seconds as they hurtled down, floor after floor.

At 'G', they stopped, a little breathless. In front of them was a keypad and door, so Jack punched in the code. There was a click. Faiza pulled the door, but it didn't open. Both boys pulled it too, but the door held fast. They looked at each other in frustration, then Jack pointed at the small notice that said *Enter Keycard Here*. They stopped pulling and stood for a second – with no keycard, how could they get out?

From far above them, came a sound that chilled them. The slamming of a door echoed up and down the flights of stairs. Holding their collective breaths, they looked up; they couldn't see anything, but they knew it wouldn't be long before Mr Blue set off some alarm and came after them. Jack pointed to the stairs that headed further down below ground and they bolted for them.

Without speaking, they ran, half-falling, down one, two, three flights, past 'B', 'B1' and even 'B2'. Finally, they ran out of stairs and all three of them stopped at the bottom, somewhat breathlessly. In the dimly lit area in front of them, they could make out a large black metal door with a single dusty rounded handle halfway up it. Next to it was a dusty sign that said something they couldn't read, and under that, 'No admittance when red light is on'. They all looked up at the dusty and broken red light bulb. With a look that said, 'There's no other way', Wade tugged at the door. It didn't budge. He pulled again, but it refused to move – it didn't have a lock or a key card slot, but somehow it had to open!

Just then everything changed. The white light flashed, turned to a pale red, and a klaxon began sounding. Clearly Mr Blue had sounded the alarm. With more urgency, Wade pulled the door again, then Jack and Faiza joined in too. After a few seconds, it gave a little and opened with a light gust of stale air. Wade jammed his foot in, pushed Jack through and signalled for Faiza to get through. She stuck her foot in the door and pushed him through, before diving through herself. The door closed very quickly with a loud metallic slam. For the second time in as many days, they had dived through a door to escape a madman and ended up in darkness.

24

The darkness was short-lived. There was a click followed by another and another as the whole area they were standing in became illuminated in a blue light. They weren't in a room; they were in a tunnel: a very long tunnel. It was about eight metres wide and the ceiling arched some four metres above them. Attached to the ceiling were lights and some metal pulleys and tracks that continued along into the dim distance. As they watched open-mouthed, the light continued to illuminate the tunnel in five-metre sections at half-second intervals far into the distance. Squinting, Faiza thought she could make out some boxes and other dark shapes at the end of the tunnel, which by her reckoning was at least three-hundred metres long!

They looked around. The blue light took some getting used to and there were a few metal benches and lockers against a wall to the left. In front of them was a half-height wall which was sectioned off every metre or so with a window-frame or a door. The frames were large and had no glass in. They crouched by a small set of lockers, still breathing heavily.

'Sis, I don't say this very often, but you were amazing up there, with that ugly blue-suited git,' said Wade. Faiza smiled.

'Well, that's what bullies need – they're not used to anyone standing up to them,' she said quietly, 'besides, he ruffled my hair and *no-one* touches my hair.'

'Frankly, it surprises me that you touch it sometimes!' said Wade laughing. Faiza narrowed her eyes.

'Shut it, Squib, or I'll feed you to Mr Blue,' she replied. 'Besides, it wasn't too clever, we're still not out yet.' She reached down to some old papers by her feet.

'Where *are* we?' asked Wade, squinting into the blue dim light.

'Oh come on!' said Faiza incredulously. 'Look around. It's obviously an old firing range.' It was Wade's turn to look incredulous.

'Wow – how do you know that?' he asked.

'The lockers, the benches, the windows without glass,' she began, 'but the biggest clue was maybe this sign on the floor that says *firing range,*' she laughed. Wade rolled his eyes.

'Do you think this was an old tube tunnel?' he asked, looking around.

'Not this bit, it's too wide, but it could be two joined together...? Maybe it splits into two down the other end?' Jack volunteered.

'Maybe we're near the old entrance to King William Street Station?' suggested Wade.

'Yeah, but it could be anywhere, as could we. We need to get out of here, and quick,' she added. There was no other door in sight, apart from the closed door behind them. Above it was a small silver panel with a red and green button. Wade turned his head to one side, stood on tiptoes, closed his eyes and pressed the green switch. There was a clicking noise from the top of the door.

'Electronic lock. Of course,' Jack said, nodding.

'At least we can slow them down getting in here.' Wade

looked back at them. 'Maybe we should check around quickly to see if there is another way out.' They tried a few of the lockers, but they were all empty. On the wall to their left was what appeared to be a list of names and months. Jack put his finger on it and scrutinised the date.

'It says December 1985 on this one!'

'And there's a newspaper here from August 2001 – the olden days!' said Wade with amazement.

'The electrics look a bit newer though.' Jack pointed at some thick cabling and trip-switches.

'Wow, how interesting,' Faiza said sarcastically. 'So here we are, deep in the earth, branded as terrorists, being chased by a blue-suited nutter and you're both interested in old papers and some electrical switches?'

Suddenly the lights, that had clicked on when they entered the tunnel, started to switch off one by one. Starting from the area in front of them, five-metre sections were systematically swamped in darkness bit by bit, until the only illuminated part was the area they were standing in.

'Nice going, Squib, look what you've done!' hissed Faiza.

'It wasn't me!' Wade protested, looking with a growing horror at the darkness.

'Hey, it must be motion detectors!' said Jack with a smile. 'How cool is that?'

'Why has it lit all the way down the tunnel then? That's miles away!' said Wade. Jack thought for a second.

'Must just turn the whole thing on the first time someone comes in.' Jack shrugged his shoulders. Faiza was about to shout for them to look for an exit, when a distant clump from the other side of the door suddenly brought their situation back into focus.

'Nuts, they found us, come on!' Wade vaulted through the open frame away from the noise, followed by Faiza and Jack in adrenaline-fuelled pursuit. As they ran down the tunnel, the lights in the section they were running into burst back into life, lighting their way. Jack was right!

No-one had been down here in a long time, judging by the amount of dust that was being thrown up. The concrete-floored tunnel tapered in a little about halfway along and the walls seemed to be less concrete and more brick. In less than three minutes, they reached the end – a dirty brick wall. The blue light lit the area but there was definitely no door this end. Breathing heavily, they crouched in the pale light and turned to face the way they had come. With a sense of impending doom, they watched as the lit tunnel they had just come along was systematically returned to darkness. Their breathing slowed and dust settled as they sat motionless. The light in their area suddenly went out.

'Do you think they will come down here?' whispered Wade.

'Depends if they can get past the electronic –' started Jack. He stopped. From the far end of the tunnel, some three hundred metres away, there was a crack of light for a moment, before it all went dark again. Then the blue light lit up the main area by the door. Someone was down there. They could hear some noises, then a distant metal clang and then silence.

'Guess they got through the door then. Have they left?' whispered Wade. It was too far away to see anything, except the blue light by the lockers. Then the blue light in the distance went out. The only sound was relief, as all three breathed out slowly.

The reprieve was short-lived. At the far end of the tunnel, there suddenly came another blue light, perhaps a little closer. Someone was still in the tunnel. Someone was still there. For a few seconds, nothing happened, and no-one moved. No-one breathed. They watched spellbound as that blue light extinguished, only to be replaced a few seconds later by another blue light just a little nearer. Someone was headed their way. Slowly. Deliberately.

25

'Don't move!' said Wade urgently and quietly. 'It'll make our area light up. There must be a way out!' Jack shook his head as they watched the next blue light go on and then go off.

'There is no way out,' hissed Faiza, anxiously watching as the blue light got slowly, but inexorably, closer. She shifted onto her other leg and the wooden board beneath her creaked. In the darkness, Jack put his head on one side. The blue light continued to go out and then go on again, getting closer and gaining in intensity.

'Oh, it can't be,' he whispered, a sense of excitement creeping into his voice. In the dark, Wade smiled; he knew that tone. Jack began rummaging around in his pocket. All the time, Faiza waited as Jack searched. Blue light on. Blue light off. Whoever it was, was now nearly a third of the way along the tunnel towards them.

'For heaven's sake, do you two have to be so slow at everything?' said Faiza frustratedly. 'We're not on a game show now – whatever you have to do, just do it!' Blue light on. Blue light off.

'He's going as fast as he can!' said Wade defensively. At that moment, Jack raised his hand and both went quiet immediately. Blue light on. Blue light off.

'Can you both shift off this board,' he said, indicating the one they were sitting on, 'and quietly put it over there. We mustn't set off the light sensors.' They didn't ask why, but feeling the edge of the board, they carefully lifted it.

Blue light off. Blue light on; getting closer. Whatever, or whoever it was, was over half of the way along the tunnel. Jack felt the area under the small board, trying not to think about the things that could be under his fingers. There it was – a recess and a small ring. He felt further out and to an edge; of something bigger. He traced it along three edges with his fingertips. Blue light off. Blue light on; closer. Using the tail of the metal Spitfire he fished from one of his many pockets, he edged it along the crack scraping out the dirt from decades of being shut. Blue light off. Blue light on.

In the distance, they could see two large shadows in the blue light. Faiza estimated they were around just over a hundred metres away now. They weren't speaking and appeared to be shining a torch left and right as they moved slowly towards them. Jack passed the wing to Wade and pulled the ring, as Wade dug into the crack. Faiza dug her fingernails into the edge too and pulled. A gust of cool stale air met them. Blue light off. Blue light on, closer and closer. Where did the hole they had just uncovered lead to?

'Just slide through and hold on, it might be a few metres down,' whispered Jack. Blue light off. Blue light on, closer.

'I'll go first this time,' said Faiza quickly, and slid through. She held onto the edges and stretched out before dropping away. 'This had better not be a sewer!' They held their breath. There was a quiet thud and she whispered up, 'I'm ok – it's about three metres. Come on!' Blue light off. Blue light on, closer and closer – the blue light was now fifty metres away. Wade tapped Jack and indicated for him to go. Jack looked at him and shook his head.

'Just go!' he hissed at Jack. Jack shook his head.

'Let's go together!' They slid their legs over the edge. 'Hang on. He pulled the wooden board back over them and counted. 'One… two…'

'Hang on!' whispered Wade. 'Do we go on three or after three?' Blue light off. Blue light on, closer and closer and closer now.

'*After* three!' Jack almost sounded annoyed. Blue light off. Blue light on, even closer. 'One… two… three!' And they both fell.

It closed behind them with a light whoosh and the wooden board slid back into place. Less than ten seconds later, the whole place was flooded with a pale blue light. Two burly men scoured the area with piercing eyes and bright metal torches. They kicked boxes out of the way and banged the walls. Neither of them thought to look at the dust-free board beneath their feet. One of them coughed. There was a crackle of static and the radio squawked, 'Mike Papa come in.' The man plucked it from his belt and pressed the talk button.

'Mike Papa receiving, over,' he announced authoritatively into the radio.

'Did you find them?' came the tinny voice.

'Erm, no sorry, sir. They didn't come this way,' replied the man. His friend continued looking around in the pale blue light.

'Are you sure? We can't find them anywhere else in the building. You'd better be damned sure,' came the reply.

'We searched the whole tunnel in the old range, but there's no sign of them.' There was a pause before the radio voice replied.

'Right, check along the whole tunnel again before sealing it and coming back up to the ground floor. We've got some terrorists to find.' The radio clicked off and the man mumbled something to his partner about being on a wild goose chase on a Sunday. They headed back along the tunnel, their way lit by a pale blue light that got paler and further away as time moved on.

26

Three metres below the board, the trio stood in the darkness looking up and listening to the muffled footsteps fade. They had landed in another tunnel, almost identical to the one they had just left, but smaller – around three metres in diameter – and dirtier. This tunnel had been abandoned for an even longer time. The dust from the ceiling continued to settle as Jack spoke.

'Honestly Wade! *On three or after three*?' said Jack incredulously.

'It was a proper question – what if I'd have gone before you? You'd be being interrogated right now!' whined Wade.

'You tell 'im, Wade's friend – he's such a clot sometimes!' Faiza laughed, more out of relief than anything else.

'You can be quiet too. If it wasn't for me and Jack, we'd all be being interrogated at gunpoint right now,' said Wade unhappily.

'Oh, I see – well if it wasn't for me, Squib, you'd all be still in that room being touched up by Mr Blue!' replied Faiza kicking the dirt by their feet.

'Look, we're here!' said Jack with a degree of finality.

'Where is *here* anyway?' said Faiza. They had been

there a few minutes and although the place was almost completely dark, they could make out slight shapes in the darkness.

'I think I know,' said Wade, 'so shall I tell you?' he teased.

'That would be nice – sometime today,' she replied in that sarcastic tone.

'We are in the King William Street tunnels,' he began. 'Remember earlier – there were two of them, but instead of running next to each other like most tube tunnels, they ran on top of each other!' They couldn't see it, but Jack was nodding.

'So,' cut in Faiza, 'the one we just dropped out of was what? The top one?'

'Yeah must have been,' said Wade, feeling the bolted framework of the tunnel. 'Looks like no-one's been down here for decades!' continued Wade.

'If they keep looking for us up above, they might find us – we should go,' said Faiza, with a sense of urgency.

'At least we can see a little bit,' said Jack as he looked towards where he thought the end of the tunnel was.

'I'll go first – hold onto my jacket' said Wade with renewed confidence. Faiza grabbed Wade's jacket and Jack held onto Faiza's.

'Careful, Wade's friend – this might mean we're married!' said Faiza laughing. Jack just tutted – partly in annoyance, partly in panic. With their hands outstretched they edged along the wall.

'Hang on, what are these?' About twenty metres further along from where they had dropped in, Wade picked up a small object. It was one of several that were around their feet, and he held it up trying to see what it was. It was about twenty centimetres long and had a glass front. Jack took it from him and turned it over several times. Wade stepped back, trying to see more in the darkness.

'It's a lamp of some kind I think,' said Jack. He flipped a switch, but unsurprisingly nothing happened.

'There's a few more here,' said Faiza, trying not to tread on them. 'Oh well, come on!' Faiza reached out for Wade's jacket, but there was nothing there. 'Wade, hang on, where are you?' she called out. There was no reply. 'Wade, this isn't funny anymore!' Her voice echoed a little, but there was still no reply. Both Jack and Faiza stumbled in opposite directions for a few steps, waving their arms a little, before slowly walking back.

Faiza was about to shout again when she heard a voice. A faraway voice that was calling her and Jack's name. It was Wade.

'Where are you, you twonk?' asked a relieved Faiza in the darkness. A few metres in front of them, there came a light clanking sound and Wade appeared to come out of the wall, with a big grin on his face.

'You won't believe what I've found!' he exclaimed excitedly.

27

Digging his fingernails into an edge, Wade pulled back a blackened, corrugated-iron sheet, that led into a large dimly-lit area. It seemed bright after the darkness of the tunnel and they were surprised to see that the whole place was a long-abandoned tube station. At the far end, sitting on the rails, was a large, dark shape covered by a grimy sheet. The metal closed back soundlessly.

'Well, what do you think of this then?' Wade said proudly, as though he had crafted the station from his bare hands. The curved platform was dimly lit by some bulbous lights hanging from the ceiling. It had a ghostly unreal feeling to it. The platform was formed of long planks of wood, on which were wooden benches that no-one had sat on for a very long time. The wall next to the platform was made of a white shiny brick with adverts and directions to the ticket office or toilets. On the opposite wall were large full-height advertisements for things Wade had never heard of, including amazing slogans like *Viking Milk – it will make you strong* and *Buchanan Furniture – you'll want to sit on it forever.*

'So *now* where are we?' asked Faiza as she stepped over the rails. All her experience told her to avoid treading on them, even though she knew there would be no current in them.

'It looks like a museum! Don't tell me we've wandered into the Transport Museum?' said Wade. Jack shook his head and explained.

'I think it's one of those disused stations we heard about. Can't be *King William Street* though – that's the other side of the river.' Jack looked along the wall where the name of the station usually appeared. There was the usual London Underground roundel, but the blue name-plate inside it was empty. They pulled themselves up onto the platform and stood looking along the length.

'Smells like that old supply teacher we had last month,' said Wade wrinkling his nose up.

'Amazing. Astonishing!' Jack said wide-eyed. He reached the bench and picked up a newspaper. 'I'll bet the last time someone was down here was early September 1940!' Faiza looked at him suspiciously, until he sheepishly held up the paper. It was very similar to the one they found yesterday at Bank, but this one was dated 8th September 1940.

'This place is ancient – like someone just forgot it. Look at these adverts!' said Faiza, running her finger along an advert for *Powys Bedding*. On it there was a picture of a woman smiling excitedly, as she stood replacing her grey sheets with spotless, impossibly white sheets!

'Have we been through a time machine?' asked Wade, as they walked further on.

'Spoken like a true geek,' commented Faiza.

'Either that,' said Jack, 'or this is one of those stations that they just built and never ended up using. We must be at the south side of the river now, near to London Bridge.' One sign stood out: *To Stairs to London Bridge Great Eastern*.

'If that's the exit,' said Faiza, indicating the arrowed sign, 'we could just head out here and count ourselves lucky.' She headed past the sign and into the darkened recess that looked like it once led to stairs. She came out a second later. 'It's blocked up; someone bricked it up a long time ago.'

'We'll have to stay a little longer then!' said Wade excitedly.

They walked a little further along the platform, small puffs of dust rising where they trod. Wade stuck his head in a room marked *Private*. Apart from over half a century of dust, there were shovels, jacks, poles and lamps.

'Wish there was a toilet too,' said Wade absent-mindedly.

'Reckon we should have a look under that sheet?' She indicated the looming grubby sheet covering something large that stood at the far end of the platform.

'I just bet that that is a carriage and I bet it's full of gold!' said Wade, bursting into a run. Faiza and Jack followed and despite their eye-rolling, they were walking quite fast too.

About two thirds of the way along, just before the mystery under the sheet, the platform abruptly ended as though someone had scooped out a huge chunk of it. Inside the deep pit were a lot of tangled metal struts and other ironmongery. There was also an open and empty battered suitcase sitting on what looked like a scruffy pile of clothes. All three of them edged towards it.

At the edge of the pit was a cap and Wade stopped to pick it up. It was black with a peak and had a badge in the middle that said *London Transport*. Wade put it on.

'Mind the gap, ladies and gentlemen please, mind the

gap,' he said, pretending to blow a whistle. Jack and Faiza laughed.

'What is all that in the pit? It looks like the Iron Man's house!' asked Faiza.

'They've got the same furniture as him anyway!' laughed Wade. He stretched out a leg and pushed one of the pieces of metal. It fell over to one side, making a dull, clanking noise and moving some of the metalwork and clothes.

'You know what this probably means don't you?' said Jack, nodding.

'Something to do with storing gold?' said Faiza rolling her eyes. 'See you're not so clever – even I got that one!'

Jack smiled and moved further along to the left of the pit. *What was that?* he thought, as he screwed his eyes up and peered further into the pit. Suddenly he did a double-take and turned back ashen-faced.

'Wade, take the hat off,' he hissed. 'Take it off *now*.' Wade looked at him, as Faiza looked over the edge too.

'Gerroff, I saw it first – it's mine!' he said proudly and put his hand on top of his head. He looked at Jack, and then Faiza, and slowly, reluctantly, he followed their gaze down towards the pit. There at the bottom, by the pile of clothes, was a jacket sleeve, and poking out of the end was a grubby, skeletal hand.

28

Wade threw the hat to the ground and kicked it away, as though it had some terrible contagious disease. All three stood transfixed, staring at the bony fingers. Breathing quickly Jack said:

'What is it?'

'What do you mean, *what is it?* It's a CD player, what do you think it bloody is?' said Faiza with more than a degree of exasperation, tinged with nervousness. Jack knew what it was, it was just he didn't want to believe it.

'No, I mean, who – whose hand is it?' Jack stammered.

'Oh wow, a real-life skeleton hand! That's so cool,' Wade said enthusiastically.

'We should get out of here, this place gives me the creeps,' said Jack, looking around him and suddenly feeling very uncomfortable.

'Do you reckon the rest of it is down there too, under those clothes and rags?' Wade was still very keen to find out.

'Duh – probably, unless skeletons go around leaving bits of themselves everywhere,' quipped Faiza.

'Could be a second-hand sale!' added Wade and laughed, but stopped when the others just looked at him.

'Wait a minute, look, is that something on one of the

fingers?' Faiza pointed down. On the index finger was something small and metallic.

'I'll go down and get it!' said Wade excitedly. Faiza and Jack shook their heads emphatically.

'No way, who knows what could be down there – all that metal; you could end up looking even worse than you do now!' Faiza said. Jack clicked his fingers.

'I've an idea – wait here a sec.' Jack ran back to the cupboard and after a few seconds of rummaging and clanking, emerged with a metal pole with clips at either end. 'I think they used this for getting things off the line.' He handed it to Faiza, but Wade snatched it from her and began aiming it towards the bones. Faiza and Jack held their breath and watched as he poked around it. Then he managed to snag the sleeve. He pulled it a bit too quickly, and it fell back revealing more of the skeleton's arm up to the elbow. A few of the other rags moved too, exposing a grinning skull.

Wade let out a yelp of surprise and almost dropped the pole. He aimed it again and this time, it caught under a band on the wrist. Slowly, and with careful movements, he pulled the bony cargo over the edge and dropped it at Faiza's feet. Unconsciously, both she and Jack took a step back before giving Wade a round of applause.

When they saw the hand wasn't about to attack them, they approached it, though still warily. Jack stayed standing, whilst Faiza and Wade went down on one knee to look at it close-up. The metallic band was exactly that – a silver ring. Wade reached out and managed to easily slide it off the bony finger. He rubbed the flat side of it and said loudly:

'Aha! Jack – look!' Jack screwed his face up a little

but moved closer. He looked hard at it for a second and nodded.

'Who'd have believed it? Another puzzle piece slips into place,' Jack said incredulously. Faiza looked at him, then at Wade, then back to Jack.

'For heaven's sake, Geek Squad! What have you found out?' she screeched. Her voice echoed off the walls and along the platform.

'The ring. The ring?' Wade replied. 'It's the same one Plum had on in that picture of him – remember the one with the backwards C?' Faiza thought hard and opened her eyes wide.

'Wow, you're right!' said Faiza. It was her turn to be amazed. 'So, who is this? Or rather who *was* this?'

'No idea. Can't be the driver – we know he died by the Thames years after that newspaper,' said Wade sadly.

'I might know,' Jack said quietly. They both looked at him. 'Well, remember that picture of the driver – there was a cap and a shadow behind him. I reckon he's the engineer or something like that. They would have needed someone else to pull this off. Pull up his coat – I bet we can find out!'

'Ugh, do we have to? This is gross,' said Faiza looking away. Wade laughed and managed to hook the coat easily enough. It was a little heavier as unfortunately it contained most of the rest of the skeleton. The skull and one of the legs became detached as he tried to lift it though and even Wade had a slightly nauseous look as it clattered onto the platform.

29

The uniform looked like that of a train guard. There was no badge on the front of the overcoat, but an attached whistle had the name of '*M Greengage*' engraved in it. Faiza got as close as she dared – two metres – and read the name out.

'He must have been the driver's assistant as you said,' said Wade eventually. 'I wonder why he never made it out of here?' Jack looked at the coat and pointed the pole at just below the top of the right-hand column of gold buttons, where his heart would have been. There was a small, ragged hole, the edge of which was darker than the rest of the material.

'Reckon the driver or Plum didn't want to share the gold and he was encouraged to give up his share,' said Jack eventually. It suddenly felt a little colder around them.

'Listen, Jack is right, let's go see that carriage thing and then get out of here,' Faiza said, feeling a little less confident. 'Can you – erm – put it back in the hole?' She picked up the hat, as Wade used the pole again to gently hoist the coat back into the hole. The skull continued to stare upwards at them from the bottom of the pit as she leaned over and dropped the hat onto the coat, followed by the silver ring. They briefly stood in silence – partly out of respect, partly out of fear – before slowly heading around the pit and further towards the mystery carriage-shaped sheet.

'If there's any more skeletons under this, I'm going to leave you here!' whispered Faiza as they reached the manky covering.

'I'll check!' said Wade lifting it gently. Decades of dust and dirt filled the air as the sheet slid right off the carriage and slipped down between it and the platform. 'Oops,' he said, coughing a little.

'Softly does it, eh?' said Faiza, waving her arms about. As the dust cleared, they could see what the sheet had been covering. They had seen it before. It was the carriage they had seen in the picture; the very one that had been used to transport the gold.

It still looked just like a sinister version of a standard train carriage – all matt black with dust and narrow slits. The difference between it and the picture they had seen was that on this carriage the doors were open and inside was…

'Nothing. There's nothing in here,' came Wade's slightly whiny voice as he climbed in, 'except a pile of paint tins.' Jack, and then Faiza, gingerly made their way in and looked round the shadowy silent interior. They walked from one end to the other, scuffling their feet on the floor and feeling the walls. It was true, all there was inside were some empty pots and a few scraps of blackened paper at the far end.

Jack lifted a pot up and read the label *'Flatlux paint'* and *'Whiter than white'*. Cogs started turning in his head, as all three of them stepped back onto the platform.

'You know, Wadey,' said Faiza flatly, 'I really thought for a second we'd found it! I almost believed. It is the right carriage, isn't it?'

'Yeah,' said Wade, 'or one that looks identical to it. I found these scraps of papers in there too – some of them are burned, but I reckon this writing on them must mean something.' Faiza snatched one from him.

'It says…' Her shoulders slumped. 'It's another code. You can tell this Plum bloke worked in the spy business! It says *070940 LBH 0114 Clink 0152 M21666 0256*. Well. What does that mean, Mr and Mr Boffin?' she asked, waving the paper in front of them.

'I've got one too,' said Wade. 'Oh, but it's just a picture of the moon and the letters HT… But this one says *070940 11:33* and it's circled, Jack? Jack?' They both turned and looked at Jack, who was now out of sight. Walking along the outside of the carriage, they found Jack pondering over two lots of metal shelving on their side. Together they pulled one of them from the track area and put it on the platform.

'What is it?' asked Wade, poking it. The rusty ironwork stood over a metre tall and half a metre wide. There were two sets of nine shelves at specific intervals along its height, each of which had twenty-eight small trays in. Jack poked it with his finger and looked back at the pit.

'I can see the stuff over there to move it. This –' she indicated the five hundred trays '– must be where they took the gold from.'

'Spot on, so what we have here is a lot of pieces of a jigsaw that's just got bigger,' said Jack sitting on the edge of the platform, wishing he had brought some lunch.

30

Faiza and Wade looked at each other, shrugged their shoulders and sat next to him.

'And what do those new bits of paper mean?' asked Faiza.

'Maybe together we can work it out – remind me what we know so far?' said Wade.

'Well, it looks like Plum arranged the route for the gold then, what – paid for a dodgy driver and his mate to drive it?' asked Faiza.

'Yes, must have. But how did they get the gold off the train in the short time?'

'That's the clever bit, and it's an educated guess really, but what we've seen the last few days does kind of back it up,' said Jack tantalisingly. After a suitable pause, in which Faiza rolled her eyes, Jack continued;

'We know they had a secret old service room at Bank where they obviously planned and plotted the thing. I suspect that's also where they kept the dodgy train guard – *Greengage* – before the gold was shipped. Plum must have been planning this for months!'

'How did they get the gold from the train then?' asked Wade.

'Well, they didn't, not really. They just *swapped carriages*.

They diverted the train from the new tunnel to London Bridge and went along these old tunnels. When it got to near here, they slowed it and unhitched the gold carriage, switching the points to this platform,' said Jack. Wade and Faiza listened, nodding.

'Could have been done with split-second timing – yeah, those reports said the train slowed at one point. And of course, there weren't any windows, just those slits,' said Wade nodding.

'Why didn't the soldiers see any of it?' asked Faiza.

'Well, again it's just based on what we've found, but I think that *friend* of the driver got out near where we got in here, changed the points and waved those lights past the soldiers so it looked like they were still moving.'

'Hmm, that could work – what, and then the driver moved it on a hundred metres and connected the empty but identical carriage to the train again!' said Wade, with excitement.

'That would be my guess too. It gave them time to unload the gold at leisure,' explained Jack.

'And when the train got to London Bridge, the soldiers could all swear that the train hadn't stopped and so the gold had just disappeared!' continued Wade all wide-eyed.

'And the gold was just taken off and shipped some-where?' asked Faiza.

'Well, Plum died a few days or so later and never told the driver – *Damson* – where the gold was, which is why he lost his mind, knowing it was out there somewhere.'

'I would imagine that Plum met *Greengage* down here the next day or so – maybe the 8th like the newspaper says – and did away with him to make sure he didn't get his share.'

'When did Plum die?' asked Faiza.

'That was not long after, so he must have been going

back to where the gold was to get it or check on it or some-thing…?' replied Jack.

'So, we can presume the gold is somewhere within walking distance of there?' Faiza looked at Jack as if to confirm.

'Yeah, but where?' asked Jack.

'I hope it wasn't just dumped in the river – we've come so close!' moaned Wade.

'No, he wouldn't do that, he'd planned it all to the smallest detail. He had to put it somewhere that could easily be taken to and from, but that no-one would see,' replied Jack confidently.

'And why were empty white paint cans in there?' said Wade suddenly, looking over towards the carriage.

'So many questions we can't answer yet. Can we get out of here now?' said Jack unhappily. 'Who knows where Mr Blue and his goons are! I bet they are all above us right now looking for us terrorists!'

'You're right, let's get out of here,' said Faiza. Jack smiled, put the pieces of paper in his inside pocket and walked round the back of the carriage. Taking a last look, Faiza and Wade walked along the curving track into the darkness towards where they thought London Bridge sta-tion must be.

'Come on, Jack, or the ghost of Greengage will get you!' shouted Wade back into the darkness. A few seconds later Jack caught them up still looking a little wide-eyed.

Twenty metres further on, they emerged back into the main tunnel. They held onto each other's coats and walked along the tunnel in almost complete darkness. Faiza led the trio and every few metres she threw a small stone in front of them. After a few minutes she stopped.

'What's up, Fize?' asked Wade a little worriedly.

'Brick wall, a few metres ahead,' she whispered. They edged forward and she ran her hands up and down it. 'I think we're trapped.'

'I really do *not* want to go back the way we came!' said Wade nervously.

'Hang on, can you hear something?' Faiza's voice came urgently. They felt an increasing movement of warm greasy air and heard a rumbling noise getting louder. It was a train; a London Underground train.

31

All three of them stopped, turned, and put their backs to the wall. The sound of a train grew, and with it came an increasing rumbling that seemed to come from everywhere. For a few seconds they froze in panic. The fear was that a train's light would come hurtling through the darkness towards them. They could feel air rushing around their faces. Then the sound and rumbling subsided and all was quiet again.

'What is this – invasion of the invisible trains?' said Faiza, more than a little relieved.

'Hang on, I've found something. It's like a clothes-airer or something,' said Wade. Faiza and Jack walked towards Wade's voice, hands outstretched. They rested their hands on a cold metal frame which was over to the right side of the wall. Wade reached down and instead of the usual concrete floor, there was an oblong recess about fifteen centimetres deep. At the bottom was a grille and through some small-bored holes in it, they could see some light three metres below. He reached along the grille and found a small handle.

'Give me a hand here,' All three of them leant through the bars and got their fingers under the grille. It was heavy, but they managed to lift it. Together they propped it up on one of the small bits of brick near the wall. Wade peered through.

'What's there, Wade – where are we?' whispered Faiza.

'It's a platform – we're at a tube station; a real modern one – looks busy,' replied Wade, craning his neck.

'My guess is London Bridge – that map we saw showed the old tunnels crossing the new ones and I think this must be where they lead!' said Jack trying to get a look.

'Let's see if we can lift it higher.' Faiza pulled at the grate and the others joined in. There was more dust as the hinge squeaked and gave a little resistance, followed by a gust of air. Beneath the grille was a recess about fifty centimetres deep and then another grille; this one with smaller holes.

'I'll go first,' whispered Wade. 'Just be careful when you land and head to the cross corridor.'

'That CCTV is a bit of a worry – it's everywhere!' said Faiza.

'Yeah, if we're quick, we should make it. There are lots of people down there, which could be bad or could be good,' whispered Wade.

'Good luck mate,' said Jack. Wade poked his feet, then his legs, into the hole and lowered himself down slowly. Quickly, he dropped down the remaining metre and darted into the side corridor. There was a murmuring from a few other passengers nearby, including an exclamation from an old woman. Thankfully most of the other people on the platform were more interested in themselves or their mobile devices. The orange LED sign indicated the next train to *High Barnet* was only one minute away. He waited and watched as he saw Jack's feet appear, followed unsurprisingly by his legs and the rest of him. He hung for about a second before dropping down and joining Wade.

The crowd of onlookers was growing though, especially when they realised there was still another person up there.

'Come on, girl!' shouted one. They watched as she too gradually emerged from the hole and hung down. She let go and dropped just ten centimetres. Her coat caught the catch at the end of the air duct. With her downwards momentum suddenly stopped, she flipped 180 degrees and hung upside down, like a panicking albatross.

'Don't just stand there, help me down!' she hissed. Two tourists took pictures of Faiza's gymnastics as Wade and Jack ran to help free her. Then there was a ripping sound and Faiza landed on them both. Helped by the other bystanders, the trio got up rapidly and dusted themselves down with the air full of thanks and apology. Looking around furtively, they ducked out of sight through one of the side corridors and into the main corridor, as the people on the platform congregated and looked up at the now closed gap in the ceiling.

'*Just get out of sight quick,* indeed,' mocked Wade.

'Shut up and let's get out of here.'

'We'll just get on the southbound train and head back to Stockwell,' said Wade. He was about to add that they should probably split up when the next train came in with the usual gust of air.

They went to join the crowd moving to get on the train, when Jack held onto Wade's coat.

'We've been rumbled!' he whispered. Faiza and Wade both looked up and at first spotted nothing amiss. Then the truth shone through in a blaze of neon colours – there now were at least twenty-five people in bright orange, yellow and pink jackets amongst the crowds of people. They were not boarding though, just looking intently at the people around them. The three crouched by the stairs.

'We can't go that way then,' moaned Faiza.

'Let's head up and out!' replied Jack. 'We could reverse our jackets and try to look a bit different.' Jack turned his inside out. Faiza and Wade did the same and all three of them made attempts at changing their hair.

'Your hair always looks like you crawled backwards through a hedge!' laughed Wade.

'And what do you call that curly mop on top of your head? We'll meet by the far side of Southwark Cathedral by the river!' she said determinedly. Seeing Wade's face however, she added; 'You can't miss it – big churchy thing. Wade, you head that way first, go!' she pointed to the closest exit and Wade shot off.

'I'll go to the Jubilee line and head up and out that way – the Borough High Street entrance,' said Jack, and he was gone.

32

Is there more staff around than usual? thought Faiza as she made her way upstairs. There did seem to be more staff in Hi-Viz jackets, but thankfully none that seemed to be paying attention to her. Looking up only when she had to, she passed through the gates and heard a bleeping sound. The gate flashed up with *Error Code 25*. She realised too late that she was trying to check out with her Zip Oyster, but it had not checked into the Underground system. She looked around straight into the face of an orange-vested woman standing by the luggage gate.

Jack strolled along a large open corridor, then headed towards the well-signposted *Borough High Street* exit. As people jostled past him, he began wondering if this place was ever empty of people. Oddly there wasn't much noise, just occasional distant murmuring and sounds of footfalls on different surfaces.

Wade was heading up an escalator. He looked across and up at the opposite escalator and held his breath as he saw a man in a pink jacket. The man appeared to be looking up and down at all the people on his escalator. Wade made no sudden movements and tried to look as casual as possible.

Then the man looked back at Wade and cocked his head ever so slightly to one side. Wade immediately turned his head and faced forward, not daring to look back behind him.

Luckily for Faiza, the helpful gate attendant woman called her over. The woman took the Zip Oyster from her and looked at it, then Faiza. She shrugged and opened the gate.

'Your jacket is inside out,' said the woman, smiling still. Faiza thanked her and headed on through, breathing a silent sigh of relief. Joining a hundred others heading in her direction, she headed out and veered left into Tooley Street. In front of her, she could see the spires of Southwark Cathedral.

The escalator Jack was on reached the top and he casually stepped off, sticking close to an old couple, one of whom was wheeling a pushchair with a small toddler asleep in it. Pretending not to notice, he held loosely on to the side of it. The couple didn't notice and talked in an American accent about whether to go and see HMS Belfast first or the Cathedral. The attendant waved them all through. After the gate, the American with the pushchair stopped.

'Hey, buddy, can I help you?' He seemed a little annoyed.

'Oh, sorry, mate, wrong pushchair.' Jack gave a smile, which was more of a grimace, and headed off, successfully getting lost in the crowd as the couple shrugged their shoulders.

Wade walked the last few steps to the top, remembering to tut as people blocked his way. He boldly stepped towards the gates and allowed himself a quick glance to the right; he could just make out a man in pink. Just then, the man turned and looked directly at Wade with a determined look on his face. Wade got close to a man in front and he scooted through the rapidly closing gates. He chanced a quick glance behind him and could see two orange-vested men coming through the gates and a pink-vested one pointing in his direction.

Following the signs for Borough High Street, Jack headed out into the sunshine, crossed the road, and headed towards the Cathedral. He saw Faiza head down some steps and, without acknowledging her, did the same thing some twenty seconds later. *At least she had made it out*, he thought, *let's hope Wade did.*

Wade was anxious. Turning left up a steel staircase in what obviously used to be a bridge arch, he was on a higher level right next to the Shard. He continued to mingle in amongst the tourists and other people criss-crossing the paths and roads. As he walked and crossed the road, he took his jacket off and reversed it so it was now the right way again. He took some steps leading down to a smaller, quieter road, and followed an old couple with a pushchair. He offered to help them with the pushchair, but for some reason they just looked at him and tutted. The Cathedral was now on his left, so he turned right and stopped by a wall overlooking the Thames.

The Cathedral is so cool, thought Faiza as she headed through it and up the stairs, dropping a pound coin in the '*rehanging the bells*' appeal barrel. She passed a small gift shop, and as she reached outside, she could see some tourists milling about the wall by the river.

33

Where had Faiza vanished to? One moment she was right in front of Jack, then she had gone. He headed round past some vendors selling beautiful-smelling hot food, reminding him painfully that he hadn't eaten for quite some time now. Ahead of him was a small area at the front of the Cathedral, where he could see lots of other tourist-type people. He approached two young people looking out across the river. They both turned around and smiled. There was almost a hug before all three stood apart, still smiling.

'Phew we made it eh! Two oranges almost got me and –' started Wade excitedly.

'Did they follow you?' asked Jack quickly, looking around worriedly.

'I don't think so, I managed to lose them in –'

'Yeah yeah, we were all almost chased by Mr Blue and his friends. Let's hope we're safe now,' said Faiza, cutting him off and pretending to be braver than she was.

'Which of those buildings do you think we were in?' asked Wade looking at the buildings across the river. On the other side, a police launch was heading upstream.

'It must be that one I reckon,' said Faiza tonelessly,

pointing out a dark-windowed, squat-looking building to the left of the bridge. Jack suddenly opened his eyes wide.

'We need to get out of here, now!' Jack's sudden and urgent tone made both Faiza and Wade look around in fear, but they could see nothing near them.

'What, what is it?' said Faiza, still looking anxiously. Jack started to walk away from the river towards the Cathedral.

'CCTV – remember in that interrogation room, we saw CCTV of us on the bank? I can see that camera from here – it could be pointing at us now!' The other two needed no further telling and ran with Jack along the small road.

'We should walk separately,' said Faiza as they carried on along the cobbled street. They split up; one on either side of the passageway and Faiza about five metres in front. They walked for a few minutes pretending to be interested in different things, but all the time looking about themselves. Wade and Jack caught up with Faiza – she was grinning from ear to ear. Behind her and to the right was a big sign; *The Clink Prison Museum*.

'Well would you look at what I found!' she said, pointing to the big red and black sign about the imposing portcullis doors. 'It said Clink on that paper we found.'

'Brilliant Fize, looks like it's not just me that's a genius then!' Wade grinned.

The three of them stopped and paused by some chairs outside a place that claimed to be the oldest pub in London. They made sure they could not be seen from the other side of the river as they sat down. It felt safer here.

'We're so close, I know it!' said Wade.

'You always say that!' countered Jack still looking around. He took the pieces of paper out.

'What have we got so far then, Jack?' asked Wade a little too enthusiastically. He read out the string of numbers and letters; '*070940 LBH 0114 Clink 0152 M21666 0256.*'

'Well I think the references to 0940 are September 1940 – so that must mean the 7th.' The other two nodded in an '*I'm impressed*' way…

'Nice going, both of you,' said Faiza. She meant it. There were a few moments of silence, as they pondered the rest of the puzzle. There was what sounded like a distant rumble.

'Why don't we get something to eat? C'mon, I can't be the only one to be hungry!'

'I'm amazed,' said Faiza.

'At what?' asked Wade.

'That you came up with a good idea!'

'Why is everyone always chasing us?' Faiza said after a few seconds. 'Thanks to you two geekoids, all I've had this weekend is lies, mud, threats, crud, chases and dark, stupid tunnels!' she said with some venom.

'Don't forget big piles of poo!' added Wade, nudging Jack.

'And dead people!' said Jack in all seriousness. Faiza narrowed her eyes and just looked at them.

'How come you two aren't bothered by this?' she asked. 'I'm serious, why are you two all happy and like kids in a sweetshop?' Wade and Jack exchanged glances.

'I guess that's it – it really feels like a real adventure,' Wade replied. 'You know what it's like at home; all saving, saving, scrimping for money, living hand to mouth in our little house,' said Wade, as Faiza just looked at him. He continued; 'Don't *you* want some excitement?'

'Yeah, I guess, but that's most people's lives, isn't it?' she said. 'If we were sensible, we would just head home and face the music or hide under our bed.'

'We can't do that. Imagine how we'd feel, giving up this close!' said Wade, a hint of exasperation creeping into his voice.

'I never knew you had so much enthusiasm – you're either really stupid or brave,' she said quietly. Wade almost turned a darker shade and just looked at the table. 'Maybe you're right. What would happen if we did the easy thing and just gave up now and went home?' She let the question hang in the air for a few moments.

'I suspect it would be the biggest regret of our lives,' said Jack suddenly.

'You're so right. We can't head home now!' said Faiza, as the others nodded. 'Besides I want to get revenge on that Mr Blue or whoever he is.'

34

'Let's look at that again,' said Faiza after a few more moments of silence. Jack handed over the paper and she looked hard at it. 'So, there's the Clink and 0152 could be –' Just then they heard the distant bells of Big Ben chiming out the hour.

'That's it!' said Jack uncharacteristically loudly again. 'Those figures – 0152 – it must be the time; eight minutes to two in the morning!'

'You're a genius!' said Wade patting his friend on the back.

'What is *LBH* then if it was earlier at fourteen minutes past one a.m.?' asked Faiza.

'London Bridge…' cut in Jack.

'Hospital!' said Faiza loudly and clicking her fingers.

'Hey, I was going to say that!' said Jack, although quietly.

'Sure you were,' Faiza added, with a smirk.

'So what have we geniuses come up with?' Wade looked at Jack.

'That's genii,' said Jack knowingly.

'Isn't that what comes out of a lamp?' countered Wade, with not a hint of amusement.

'Shut up,' said Faiza quickly, 'and let him continue.' She nodded at Jack to carry on.

'So, what have we got then, *Inspector*?' said Wade as Jack was about to speak. Faiza looked a little confused but listened anyway.

'Well, *Chief*, presumably something was at LBH at just gone 1:15 a.m. and at the Clink at nearly two a.m. I'm guessing that he got the gold out of one of the tunnels under London Bridge.'

'Someone would have seen it – there was a war on!' chipped in Wade.

'Good point. Well, considering the roads and Blitz conditions, I reckon they transported the gold by river, coming ashore just down here by the Clink.' He nodded over his shoulder at the small wall which bordered the Thames. Both Wade and Faiza sat wide-eyed.

'And then?' Wade dared after a few seconds.

'Well that's where uncertainty creeps in,' replied Jack looking a little crestfallen. 'It's this bit; *M21666 0256*. That 0256 must be the time, but what is *M21666*? Something seems familiar about that.' Jack scratched his head and frowned, followed moments later by the other two.

Wade, who was facing away from the river, suddenly leaned in over the table.

'Don't look, whatever you do. We need to leave. We *need* to leave.' He looked at them wide-eyed. In her peripheral vision, Faiza could make out several men emerging from under the bridge, where they had recently come from. They stood out because they were all in the same dark suits with sunglasses. They stopped and seemed to be scanning the area.

'Let's split up,' she hissed. 'One at a time, leave easily. I'll head past the Clink, Jack you head off towards that way.' She moved her eyes towards Southwark Bridge, a hundred metres to the west.

'What shall I do, just sit here?' said Wade sarcastically.

'If you like, but if I was you I would wait twenty seconds and head through that housing development.' Faiza indicated, with a finger across her chest, to the right.

'Where shall we meet?' said Wade quietly. Jack slowly and deliberately got up to leave, keeping his back to the men who seemed to be looking at everyone around the area. The three men then moved more purposefully to the pub. Two of them went in whilst another waited outside, like a mountain-sized sentry.

'Arthur Road.' And he was gone.

'What, what? Where the flip is that?' said Faiza crossly, although she knew it seemed familiar. She tried not to look where Jack had disappeared into the crowd.

'Surely a genius knows that?' Wade whispered, grinning. Faiza was about to say something devastatingly funny, when she spotted the man looking over towards the river.

'Look, they'll spot us now for sure.' She seemed despondent.

'Let me help,' he said, and slowly got up.

Pretending to look at something in his hands, Wade headed slowly towards some flats and houses. As he got to where the man was standing by the door, he stopped and looked up at him. The man was trying to speak covertly into a radio and Wade could just make out an anxious tinny voice. The man took a few moments to realise there was someone just watching him. He was about to tell the lad where to go, when he did a double take. By the time the man had stretched out his tree-branch of an arm, Wade was already several metres away and sprinting towards the houses. The man followed as fast as he could but was not nearly as successful at dodging tourists and pushchairs and dogs and children!

35

Faiza had watched spellbound and with some horror, as Wade zipped away through the crowds, followed clumsily by first one, then two more, dark-suited men. She breathed in and out slowly, hoping he would be fine but feeling helpless. She had remembered where she had heard 'Arthur Street' so knew where to go. Standing up slowly and giving the table to an anxious old couple with a pushchair, she walked back the way they had all just come, past the Clink, towards London Bridge.

Jack found that he had no problem leaving and was soon heading over Southwark Bridge. Every now and then he would stop to pretend to do his laces up but could see no-one paying him any attention at all. He also made sure he was on the far side of the bridge, away from any CCTV cameras on *that* building. Once over the bridge and keeping the river on his right, he headed eastwards towards Arthur Street.

Faiza had passed the Clink and the Golden Hinde, as well as what seemed like a million people. She did see a few grey suits and Hi-Viz jackets, but she didn't hang about to look too closely at them. Once past the Cathedral, she climbed the steps to London Bridge and headed along it in the crowds towards Arthur Street.

Wade's journey was more interesting and more energetic. He headed rapidly through the housing development and into a quiet road. Fuelled by adrenaline, he carried on pushing forward. He could still hear shouting behind him as he ran across the road, right in front of a white *Kia Sportage* moving at speed. The driver let him know what she thought of his antics, as he disappeared under a railway bridge and into a place called Borough Market.

Inside it was darker, but still very much full of people. There were green pillars and people everywhere, with a thousand different smells. As he stopped and stood panting behind a paella stand, he could see a few men in orange at the opposite end. They were looking intently into the market and crowds. Not good news. As he looked towards where he had come in, he could see more men in orange and pink arrive, as well as at least five men in grey suits. They seemed to be at most of the exits now. He was trapped.

Wade retreated further back behind the stall and looked around the area. There were a lot of boxes and spare things for the stalls. A few old men sat on an upturned crate against a green pillar and stared at Wade. Still panting, he asked;

'Is there another way out?' The men just looked at him for a few seconds, before one of them pointed with his foot towards a small alcove. Wade thanked him and slipped into the area between two pillars. The alcove was not a way out, but simply three white wooden walls. In the middle of one of them was a small red box with a glass front.

Wade carefully thought for a second and was about to march back out, when he realised that this may very well be a way out. Closing his eyes, he pulled his elbow back and hit the small red box. From everywhere at once came a loud insistent ringing. He had set off the fire alarm!

He jumped quickly out of the alcove and almost tripped on a large brown overcoat. A lightbulb appeared above his head. The coat was a little large, but it made him look like one of the porters. Trying not to look how he felt, Wade caught up with the old men. He slipped in next to them and tried as hard as he could to be one of them; occasionally looking at them and then ahead.

As he approached a large exit, he could see at least a dozen people; some in grey, some in orange, pink or yellow Hi-Viz vests. Where could he run to if they saw him? As it happened, and to his surprise, he found it much easier to get past than he thought. Looking like part of their group of four, he simply walked past them. He carried on strolling but held his breath until he was across the road from the market. Why had everyone else stopped? Of course, it must be the muster point for the fire alarm.

He stood next to the three men, thinking fast. If he suddenly moved or left, they'd surely say something or maybe even start a scene. The answer came as unexpectedly as finding that coat. One of the men, a grey-haired Asian man, leaned over to Wade and whispered.

'Give me your coat my friend and sneak out between us.' Wade looked at him wide-eyed and then at the others, who nodded. Wade felt like shaking the man's hand, but before he could give it another thought, the man added: 'We were all young once. Go.'

Wade needed no other bidding. He slipped the brown coat off and vanished between them, heading with some other tourists back towards London Bridge. He took a last look at the crowd of unhappy looking people and got to the top of the stairs onto the bridge, where he could still hear the fire alarm.

Jack had got to Arthur Street first and he waited in the blue and white mosaic subway they had gone through earlier. He waited. And waited. People paid him scant notice as they passed either to or from the stairway. Jack was just wondering whether he should head back when a hand landed with force on his shoulder.

He spun around and looked in fear at the owner of the hand, before smiling. Faiza took her hand off and laughed.

'Wow, Jack,' she said. 'You look like you need a change of underwear!' She looked past Jack and briefly around. 'Wade not here yet?' Jack shook his head. They stood in a kind of awkward silence hoping the next person they saw would be a smiling Wade. A minute passed.

'I think I've worked out that code,' he said. Faiza just stared at him.

'What? Why didn't you say? So – erm – wow, what is it?'

'And,' he said in a quieter voice, 'I'm pretty sure I know where the gold is and if I'm right, we can go and get it anytime we like – well, as long as it's within normal opening hours!'

'Oh, that's brilliant – so go on, where is it and how do we get it?' said Faiza excitedly. Jack was about to tell her when a shadow fell across them.

36

Wade had headed north over the bridge. Happily, there were plenty of other tourists to walk and mingle with. He didn't look behind and hoped that no-one was following him. Occasionally he saw a man in a suit, but he kept his cool and they walked past him. He came to the far end of the bridge and happily headed down into the blue and white mosaic subway.

Heading down the stairs, he rounded the corner at the bottom. No-one there. Wade stepped out and looked right then left, expecting to cross the road, but he stopped stock still. Just ten metres to his left, he saw three dark-suited men holding Jack and Faiza, both of whom were trying to struggle. In the road were two black cars, parked at strange angles. With his back to Wade, again, was the man in the blue suit.

'You really want me to rain down bad things on you?' spat Faiza at the people holding her, but mostly to Mr Blue, who laughed and shook his head. He winced as he remembered his bandaged head hurt.

'You are in no position to bargain, little girl, even using American TV language like that. This time I've got you,' he said slowly.

'Yeah, yeah like last time?' she hissed. 'Did he tell you that last time we met, he was beaten up by this *little girl?*' Mr Blue seemed to look uncomfortable for a second, before regaining his composure. He looked her right in the eyes.

'And who do we have here, another accomplice? So where is your other friend little man?' Mr Blue prodded Jack in the shoulder and ruffled his hoodie. 'C'mon, you look like the brains of the outfit – I doubt the other two could even tell me the colours of a traffic light. Tell me where your little friend is.' Jack looked at him but didn't say a word.

'Come on, you can do it – are you old enough to speak yet?' said Mr Blue with that greasy grin again. Jack looked up, then he began slowly whispering; 'Ten… nine…' Mr Blue craned his neck to hear and then looked at the men around him.

'What? What are you whispering? Is that a count-down?' he demanded.

'Eight… seven… six…' Jack continued, as Faiza smiled and joined in.

'So what happens at zero, little man? Little girl?' Mr Blue was beginning to get a little rattled. They didn't even seem scared – didn't they know who he was?

'Five… four…' Even the grey-suited men around them looked at each other with a mixture of confusion and mild amusement.

'Shut up, just shut up!' Mr Blue shouted at them. 'Oh, just get them out of my sight!'

'Two… they both said loudly, as the men started to march Faiza and Jack towards the car.

'Now what?' Mr Blue and his fellow henchmen laughed.

'One!' came a voice from behind them.

Mr Blue ducked, just in time to feel the swish of air above his head as a long wooden plank flew past. It hit the grey-suited man to his right, who dropped to the ground immediately. Wade was carried round with the momentum of his plank swing and let go of it slightly too late. He rolled onto his right foot, but both he and the plank fell with a clatter onto the man who had already suffered a plank-hit. Before he could separate himself from the man and the wood, a large pair of hands grabbed him and hauled him to his feet.

'Wade,' asked Faiza. 'You ok? We were waiting for you and…'

'Be quiet.' Mr Blue waved a hand in the air and Faiza fell silent. Wade nodded, then shook his head. The man with the injured head lay there still making light moaning noises. His other dark-suited friend held tightly onto Jack and started to drag him over to where Wade was standing. Very quickly Mr Blue put a hand up. The man stopped and looked right at Mr Blue.

'Stand down. They'll get theirs soon enough,' Mr Blue said in a matter-of-fact type way.

'Sorry, guys,' Wade said quietly a few seconds later. Jack nodded in acceptance.

'Only *you* could swing a plank at someone a metre away and miss – as if his head wasn't big enough!' Faiza said, turning pointedly to Mr Blue.

'If you aren't quiet, I shall make sure you stay quiet. For a long time.' His dead-eyed gaze stayed fixed on her.

'You can try, big man,' she hissed, struggling futilely once more.

'And I'll quieten your friends too,' he added, casting a glance at the helpless duo held firm.

Faiza was about to say something but closed her mouth. If looks could kill, Mr Blue and his cronies would be dust already. 'Take them to the cars and head for LPS House. You remember that?' he said facing the three again. 'That's the place we last met; the place you assaulted me. You won't get away this time.' He put his hand on Jack's shoulder.

'Hah, what about your boss?' asked Wade suddenly. 'When she finds out, she'll kick you into the Thames!'

'Oh don't worry your little heads about that. She gave me orders to keep an eye on you and, well, if you're stupid enough to try to shoot me with a gun you found, then I was only acting in self-defence.' Mr Blue smiled and shook his head.

'You'll never get away with this!' said Wade, struggling. Mr Blue laughed. It wasn't a pleasant laugh.

'If this was Scooby Doo, I might agree with you, rip off a mask and say something like *If it weren't for you pesky kids,* but it's not and you're not getting out of this.' He smiled that grim, greasy smile again and indicated with his head towards the cars. All three of them struggled, but it was no use. It was over, there was no escape this time.

37

'Zero!' shouted Wade, then stamped down hard on the foot of the man holding him. The man let go of his captive immediately and hopped backwards off-balance. Wade rushed back three metres and picked up a large bag of cement that he had left behind the car. Faiza dropped to her knees, but the man did not let go of her so she used all her strength to do a forward roll. The man's head hit the ground with a thud, and she was free. The man holding Jack threw him aside and headed for Wade. Wade held the bag above his head and threw it to the ground. The effect was instantaneous; billowing clouds of choking, blinding cement filled the air. There was a lot of indistinct shouting and coughing as visibility reduced to zero.

'I can't breathe.'

'Stop them!'

'I've got one!'

'That's my foot!'

'Where are they – stop them!'

'I've got the girl!'

'Get your behind out of my mouth'

'Don't let them escape. Whose knee is that?'

Sounds of bodies hitting bodies and metal clips and feet on the pavement; some far, some close. There was the sound of another bag of cement hitting the pavement, with more clouds and blinding dust! A car revved its engine and then cut out. More shouting and car doors slamming.

'Excellent – you've stopped them getting away in the car!' Mr Blue spluttered over the din. The noises and shouts stopped; they must have a good result! He stumbled through the clouds and walked over to the noise with arms outstretched. Slowly the cement dust began to clear. The scene that met his eyes was vastly different to two minutes earlier. The three prisoners had vanished. What he could see, through his tear-streaked eyes, were two men lying motionless on top of each other on the pavement.

They appeared to be handcuffed to each other. He made out another man who had handcuffed himself to the wing mirror of one of the black cars. Mr Blue just sighed and turned his back on the devastation. He pulled out a radio from his back pocket.

'Yes… yes… scenario seven unfortunately. Code two priority; Lockdown alert at Arthur Street. Three youths probably covered in cement dust and armed. Get a clean-up team here right away; Team 8R have failed and require assistance – code four, and you'll need bolt-cutters.' He sighed. 'Contact team 6P and tell them to be ready to move as soon as they hear from me – Bank area only. Inform Gold leader about a Code Seven in Docklands.' He switched the radio off and put it back on his belt.

From his inside pocket, he pulled out his smartphone and typed in his six-figure passcode. Activating an app called 'Kate Low', he frowned and then smiled as he watched a red dot blinking and moving across the screen.

'Sir? Sir, could you help me? Erm – I seem to be stuck.' Mr Blue looked in the direction of the voice, which belonged to the man who had attached himself to his wing mirror. Mr Blue frowned, turned on his heels and then headed off quickly towards Monument.

Four minutes later and almost three hundred metres away, Faiza, Wade and Jack sat in a small side-room in a quiet part of a church.

'That was brilliant!' spluttered Wade, trying to brush mountains of cement dust from him.

'I think I managed to handcuff one of them to the other one!' said Faiza, still coughing and laughing.

'That was amazing, Wade,' said Jack, clearing his throat. 'I thought we were finished. 'Brilliant thinking!'

'We're a good team eh?' said Wade.

'Proud of you, Bro. Anything that gets that Mr Blue angry is great!' Faiza shook her head producing small clouds of dust.

'Are they after us?' asked Jack with an ear to the door.

'I can't see from here, but I suspect not.' She went quiet as she heard a police siren nearby, but it faded into the distance.

'Don't breathe in the dust, it's not good for you,' said Jack.

'Now you tell us!' said Wade, trying to hold his breath, but failing.

'I think we may have kicked a wasps' nest,' said Jack, a little more despondent.

'We're safe for now,' said Faiza, looking around the small empty room. 'But you know what – you're right, Wade; we do make a good team.'

'Yeah, the power of three!' cheered Wade.

'Well, with your friend here, it's more like two and a half,' said Faiza laughing.

'Ah, you don't mean that. Besides its both of you that need me now,' said Jack confidently.

'What for?' said Wade.

'Because I know where the gold is now.' It was Jack's turn to have the biggest grin. 'I'll tell you on the way – c'mon it's time to go!'

38

'We'll have to head around the outside I think,' said Jack as they warily exited St Stephen's Walbrook. As they cautiously walked along a quiet back alley, Jack explained what he had worked out.

'So that last bit *M21666 0256;* well we'd already got the time bit – 0256 – but what was M21666? I thought about it then when I was walking to our meeting place, I looked upwards and saw the truth.'

'What, divine intervention?' said Wade. Faiza pinged him on the ear.

'As in Monument to 1666!' said Jack, with a well-deserved, smug grin. 'The Great Fire of London of 1666!' Wade stopped and nodded as he spoke.

'Of course! That makes sense now. So he got the gold down river from LBH – London Bridge Hospital – to the Clink then across the river to near Arthur Street. How did he transport it up the hill to the Monument?'

'Only conjecture,' said Jack, 'but a horse and cart waiting there could take it and with all the blitz and kerfuffle going on, no-one would have noticed and –' Jack stopped dead. 'No, it couldn't be. Do you think –'

'What?' the other two asked, a little perturbed.

'...that the ghost on a horse and cart that my

great-great-grandad saw, could have been Plum and his gold?' Both Faiza and Wade laughed.

'Yes, yes of course! Ah I guess we'll never know for sure, but yeah right!' said Wade loudly. Jack continued.

'He could have just painted himself white – we did find some white paint in that carriage – and no-one would have stopped a ghost in the Blitz!'

'That's amazing – that Plum was almost clever, eh?' said Wade.

'A thieving clever git who caused a lot of trouble!' cut in Faiza.

'You wait till I tell my great-great-grandad!' Jack was more animated than Wade had ever seen him.

'So this gold, these half-kilo bars of gold, whereabouts in the Monument would they be?' asked Faiza. Each was thinking the same thing – at the top.

As they approached the Monument, still keeping close to the buildings, they stopped and briefly held their breath. They ran their eyes from the top to the bottom and back again, focusing on the gold-coloured ornate workings at the top.

'That must be it!' said Wade. Jack made a face like he was chewing a wasp.

'I'm not so sure – how would he have melted the gold down and then got a crane to stick it on the top?' said Jack.

'Well anyway, let's go find out – last one up there can –' she stopped mid-sentence and rapidly pulled the other two into a small alleyway. Before they could protest, she pointed towards the base of the Monument. They followed her gaze and saw what she was looking at; two burly men walking around it. The men stopped in front of the open entrance and looked around. Then they headed off down

Fish Street Hill, towards the church where the three had been earlier.

'That's it!' Jack said excitedly. The other two looked at him. 'Look it's there – right in front of us!' Faiza and Wade looked at him incredulously. 'Plum was a git, but he was so clever. There's the gold! In plain sight of 150,000 people a year ha ha!'

'Where? Just tell us, geekoid!' said Faiza impatiently.

'You need me now eh; and the geek shall inherit the world!' he laughed. 'Come on.' All three of them started to head towards the tall white and gold tower.

'You can let go of us now, Mum,' said Wade impatiently. Faiza smiled as she realised she was still holding the shoulders of their jackets and released her grip.

'Hang on, what's that on your shoulder, Jack?' asked Faiza. Jack looked at his left shoulder and his eyes opened wide. It appeared to be a small, matt-black patch about four centimetres long, with a raised black bubble in the centre.

'Oh no, oh no!' said Jack, louder than Faiza had ever heard him speak. He started to yank his jacket off as he hissed.

'It's a tracker – we've got to go! Scatter now!' The other two looked horrified for a second, then ran out of the alley across the road past some bicycle racks. Just at that moment around the corner of the alleyway strode a purposeful Mr Blue. He clamped his hand onto Jack who was still trying to separate himself from the sleeve of his jacket and force his way past two black-suited men. Wade turned and was about to run back, when Faiza veered towards him and grabbed him bodily. She put her hand over his mouth and pulled him away, keeping him hidden from view.

39

From their vantage point they could see three more men come running from further along the small alley and another two from the Monument. Jack, who was still struggling, looked the opposite way and shouted 'Kashive! Get to the boat, get to the boat! See you at Waterloo!'

'Let go of me, we've got to help Jack!' Wade said angrily at Faiza, who refused to let go.

'We can't help him now! We'll be caught too – stay quiet!' They painfully watched Jack being bundled away down the alleyway towards the river area. Faiza kept hold of Wade as she lifted him bodily and headed away.

'Let me go, let me go!' hissed Wade, as she put him down a minute later in a side passageway behind a tree. He glared at her.

'We could have rescued him!' he whined

'What, me and you versus six mobile couches?' she replied, still holding onto him. 'Just be quiet a minute,' she said impatiently. 'Your friend, our friend, Jack, just bought our freedom!'

'What? We have to go and get him, he's –'

'He's been captured, and he's led them away from us to the river,' said Faiza matter-of-factly.

'Let's wait a few minutes and make sure it's all clear.' Said Wade quietly, accepting that Faiza was right. 'Do you really think Jack will be alright?' he added. Faiza looked at him.

'He'll be fine. Mr Blue is after me really. Oh, if his boss knew what he was really like, he'd be...' her voice trailed off as though something had just occurred to her. She smiled and then continued. 'Besides he's not likely to talk much, is he?' She nudged Wade, who laughed, and they both got to their feet.

'Right, bro, we must get to the Monument. Prove our innocence and find that gold.'

'Let's do it,' he said determinedly. 'Erm, how?' Wade asked.

'You head around that way to Monument and I'll head back the way we came. You get there in ten and I'll be there in fifteen. We'll queue up separately to go up and meet you at the top. Keep your eyes out for scary people and for gold.'

'What will we do at the top?' asked Wade.

'No idea, but if Jack could see the gold from where he was, it must be somewhere in plain sight. Let's start at the top and work down.'

'Have you – erm – got any cash, to get in?' he asked. She dug into her pockets and handed him a five-pound note. 'I'll give you back the change.'

'Damned straight you will.' She smiled.

'Good luck... sis,' he said smiling. Wade headed away slowly, then stopped and looked back, a wistful look in his eyes. She nodded slowly and silently, and he quickly disappeared.

Twelve minutes later, Faiza approached the Monument from the west. There was a small queue of people; a young couple with a toddler and two old ladies. In front of her, the two old ladies and then the family had a quick chat with the cashier, before walking away talking quietly to themselves. Now at the front of the queue, she asked him whether it was closed.

'No, madam, if you'd just like to head up.' He ushered her through the turnstile.

'Do you want me to pay?' she asked, a little confused. The man looked a little flushed for a second.

'Erm, yes that's –' he looked at the price list on the wall '– two pounds, sixty pence.' Faiza handed over the five-pound note and pocketed the change.

Wade was already on his way to the top having queued and entered five minutes earlier. 'What a view!' he heard repeatedly from people coming down as he slogged his way to the top. *It had better be a good view*, he thought, as he pushed himself up the last few steps. He stepped out through the doorway onto the concrete square platform, bordered by white metre-high railings and an overhead fence, presumably to stop items, or people, vanishing over the side.

Holding onto the railings, he could see St Paul's Cathedral, the Thames and many of the other new taller buildings that seemed to be springing up in the city. Around this side he could even make out the place where Faiza, Jack and he had sat and pondered earlier! Faiza would be here in a few minutes, so he decided to see what it was like around the other side.

From the bottom of the spiral staircase, Faiza peered up – it seemed to go on forever. She took a deep breath and started to climb. The steps were quite small so she hoped it wouldn't be too taxing. She reached the 311th step a little breathlessly as the natural light flooded the exit.

40

She stepped out onto the platform and looked out in the sunshine at the magnificent view. Her awe turned to fear as she heard a slow drawl.

'Did you lose something, miss?' It was the voice of Mr Blue. Wade half-stumbled around from the other side, with a determined Mr Blue right behind him. The look on Wade's face told Faiza everything she needed to know.

'Now I've got all three of you.' He gave her that smug grin and added. 'Ah ah – don't come any closer.'

'Wade? Wade, you ok?' Faiza looked at Wade, who was struggling a little bit in Mr Blue's grip.

'Yeah, I'm fine. He just grabbed me around the other side and –' Suddenly Mr Blue pushed Wade at Faiza.

'How's your head, Blue?' Faiza asked, helping Wade stay on his feet. Mr Blue frowned and put a hand up to his bandage.

'I'll live. You'll pay for that as well,' he snarled. He was standing squarely between them and the stairs down.

'Just leave us alone and let us go!' she hissed back at him.

'Such devastating words,' he laughed. 'If you like, you can think up some more during the next few years when you're in the Young Offenders home for idiots.'

'You know what you're going to get –' Faiza started but stopped as he held up a large truncheon from inside his long blue jacket.

'Well, I know what you're going to get if you take another step. Here – take these. He threw them some large red cable-ties. 'Now,' he urged. Wade picked them up slowly.

'Tie her wrists and make sure it's nice and tight.' Mr Blue signalled to Wade, who looked apologetically at Faiza. She nodded that it was ok, then stared back at Mr Blue. 'Tight now, y'hear.' Faiza put her wrists together as Wade clasped the cable-ties round them. 'Does that hurt, little girl?'

'Oh ow, ow,' she said sarcastically. He moved closer to her and spoke quietly.

'I suggest you stay very quiet. It would be awful if you were to take the direct route down.' He indicated towards the ground with his eyes.

'Just take these off my wrists and we'll see who is taking the quick route down,' she hissed. Mr Blue grabbed Wade and put a set of cable-ties on his wrists too.

'Where have you put Jack?' demanded Wade.

'Oh, is that what the other little one was called?' he said, nodding slowly. 'He kept insisting his name was Zac. Well he's safe and soon you'll be *safe* with him too.' The way he said 'safe' made Wade shiver inside.

'Right, well, guess it's time I charged you, so you can resist arrest. I'm going to get a medal for this.'

'Yeah, just you versus three kids. What a hero you are!' Faiza said dryly. 'You know we're innocent of everything except maybe being way younger than you!' Mr Blue's expression changed for a second.

'You're very funny. Witty almost. Anyway, what have we got on you then? You've run me a merry dance around the city, cost tens of thousands of pounds and been causing all kinds of problems. You are a public menace. You've caused car crashes, explosions, injuries to security personnel and taken part in terrorist activities.'

'That's all rubbish and you know it. I suspect the worst thing was that we made you look like the vindictive, power-mad prat you really are,' she snapped back, a fierceness growing in her eyes. Wade turned to face her fearfully.

'Faiza!' Wade pleaded. 'I know he's a you-know-what, but can you stop winding him up even more? He's going to go bonkers!'

'Going to go MORE bonkers!' Faiza hissed. Mr Blue just nodded with a knowing smile.

'And of course, I am going to add assaulting a security officer and grievously resisting arrest. I do hope you don't fall down the stairs on the way down.'

'You're threatening us too? Just let us go!' Faiza realised that struggling was pointless, as the sharp edges of the restraints bit into her wrists, making her angrier. Suddenly, his face lightened.

'Of course, I could just let you go and we could forget all about it. Call it high spirited teenage jinks?' he smiled that greasy grin again. Faiza and Wade just looked at each other, more than a little confused.

'Erm, ok?' said Wade, slowly.

'All you'd have to do, is tell me where the gold is.'

41

Mr Blue let the last few words hang in the air. Both of his captives looked at each other, a look of fear, confusion and hate on their features that they found hard to hide.

'What gold?' said Wade, after a second or two.

'You've got us confused with someone else or more likely you're confused! We don't know nothing about no gold,' hissed Faiza angrily.

'Don't try to deny it, even with your defensiveness and double negatives. I've had a tip off and I know you must have found it.' He was speaking much faster now and there was a slightly distant look in his eyes.

'I don't care what you've had off – we don't know what you're talking about. You're mad!' said Faiza. Mr Blue threw his head back and laughed.

'You must know. You do know,' Mr Blue said, as he stepped a little closer towards them.

'Even if we did know, we wouldn't tell you, you failed excuse for a wannabe spy, in an unfashionable shade of blue,' said Wade. Mr Blue stopped laughing and stared at Wade like he might explode.

'So, is it here? Is it at the top here?' he suddenly said, kicking the railings. They tried to back away from him as he continued; 'Come on, you know what gold – *Corner's*

Calamity – the gold that disappeared in the war! I've known about it for a long, long time. It belongs to me and my family!'

'Gold? Do you mean the metal up there?' Wade tried to point at the topmost part of the monument. Mr Blue looked at it and laughed dismissively.

'It's close; I can feel it!' he exclaimed. 'My great-uncle hid it somewhere and it's our birthright!' Faiza and Wade stood there open-mouthed.

'You are related to... to *Plum*?' Wade stuttered. Mr Blue looked back at them.

'Related to him? I should say so. My name is *Plum*; Henry Plum.' Faiza and Wade stood there a little dumbfounded for a moment before he continued. 'In the family, we've always known it was him – he left loads of evidence behind.'

'Ha – everything apart from where he put it!' said Faiza guffawing.

'Yeah, shame he didn't read up on things to do in an air raid, like not go out walking!' added Wade.

'We kept all the evidence hidden to save the family name, but we've been looking for our reward ever since. I think *you* know where it is.'

'Do you think we'd be talking to the likes of you if we did?' Wade was enjoying himself a little more now.

'You looked for it, you know where it is and now you're going to tell me.'

'We didn't, we don't and we're not,' replied Faiza determinedly.

'Look here, I know. And I know you know.' His left eye had started to twitch a little.

'Ah, but do you know that we know you know we know?' said Wade seriously.

'Once I heard about you on the Underground at Bank, I knew. You were looking into that code and I think you cracked it,' said Plum decisively. He reached in his pocket and pulled out the piece of paper with the code printed on it. They wondered what had happened to Jack's paper with the code on it. Now they knew.

'Still don't know what you're talking about,' said Faiza matter-of-factly.

'You do. Tell me. I need to know. Tell me and I'll set you free!' The twitch in his left eye was becoming more pronounced. They both backed away a little further from him, but he grabbed Faiza's arm.

'You're a nutter, Blue, or Plum, or whatever you're called, and you need to see someone! We don't know nothing about no gold. Let us go, you git!' screamed Faiza and she kicked him hard in the shin, but Mr Blue's grip stayed firm. He took a deep breath and grimaced but didn't let go of her.

'Two shins in one day! You know, once they find the evidence, there'll be no way out for you or your little friends, for about twenty years I reckon.'

'What evidence?' piped up Wade, continuing to try to wrestle his wrists out.

'Oh you know; tools found in your bedrooms, explosive accelerants, internet history of bomb-making sites, banned materials stolen from school and found at home – I've done it before,' he said, ushering them towards the door.

'Ah but what about when your lovely boss finds out? You're scared of her!' said Faiza, resisting his attempts to pull her closer to the exit.

'My *lovely* Boss? Miss C?' he said, laughing. 'She'll never find out – wait till she sees the evidence. As I said, she's not rumbled me before and she's off on some wild goose chase at Docklands leaving me in charge! I'm not scared of her.'

'You should be,' came a northern Irish voice from behind him.

42

Plum spun around in a state of disbelief and locked eyes with Miss Corner. For a second there was absolute silence in the world.

'Thank God you're here!' Plum said, louder than he needed to. 'I've just detained these two criminals who I believe were about to –'

'Stand very still,' she said quietly and authoritatively. No-one moved as she pulled out a radio from her inside pocket and turned it on. 'Stand down, code Tango Oscar Yankee.' A second or so later came confirmation.

'Now. Right, that's the snipers stood down. Wouldn't want them aiming at the wrong target. Mr Plum, sorry – agent Three-nine, kindly report,' said Miss Corner. Mr Plum puffed himself up and put on his most professional face.

'I apprehended one of their gang half an hour ago and he told me that they were about to plant a device up here. I quickly mobilised a force and got up here just in time.' Plum said. Wade and Faiza went to protest, but Miss Corner raised a hand, and they went instantly silent. Mr Plum smiled to himself.

'Are you two ok?' Corner looked over at Faiza and Wade who nodded. 'Well that's a small mercy for you, Plum.'

Plum looked a little taken aback, before realising what she meant.

'I don't understand. These kids were about to blow up the Monument and kill hundreds of –'

'Agent Three-nine,' she said cutting him off. 'I have been standing there for the last four minutes. I heard everything. *Everything.*' Corner emphasised the last word, which seemed very final. She continued; 'This smart girl called me less than half an hour ago and told me what you had been up to.' Corner looked over at Faiza and smiled. If Wade could free his hands, he would have clapped.

'You don't understand – I was trying to get them to admit to their terrorist activities!' He was clutching at straws now and even he knew it.

'These young people are innocent, and you will surrender yourself,' she added. 'The place is surrounded now. You can't escape.' Plum's shoulders slumped and he looked down at the ground in silence. Corner went to reach into her pocket for her radio. Then everything seemed to happen at once. Plum suddenly leapt fast at Corner. She was caught off guard as he grabbed and twisted her round. Forcefully he pushed her into Faiza and Wade, all three of whom careered onto the floor.

'I'll see you!' he shouted, as he headed towards the only door. Wade instinctively stuck his foot out and Plum's exit through the door turned into a half-run, half-stumble. There was some scuffling from the dark doorway as Wade got to his feet very quickly and hurtled after Plum.

'No, Wade!' shouted Faiza, trying to separate herself from Miss Corner. Corner sat up and grabbed her radio from her pocket.

'This is Gold leader. Code four-seven, we have a code four-seven on agent three-nine. It's Plum!' she hissed into the radio.

Wade rushed through the door. It seemed very dark, after the brightness of being outside in the sun. He didn't have time to think and he hurtled down the spiral staircase, the small windows flying past. He looked over the edge as he ran and he could see Plum's arm whizzing round and down. Wade was only two storeys above Plum but was already nearly halfway down.

Wade moved up a gear and began to take the stairs five and six at a time. It meant he was continually almost stumbling, but the circular wall was helping him stay mostly upright. He knew that Miss Corner and Faiza would be following somewhere behind and there would be lots of heavies outside, but this time they would be stopping Plum instead of helping him.

Seconds passed and Wade was getting closer now. Both were out of breath as Wade made a final lunge forward at Plum. He managed to catch the edge of Plum's boot which knocked him off balance. Plum careered into the wall, bounced off it and went headlong down at least fifteen stairs. Wade was also now falling and rolling and just as Plum was almost back on his feet, Wade barrelled into him.

Plum took another unwanted headlong dive and he head-butted the wall, before rebounding into the railings. He made a groaning sound as his head shot between them. He slumped down to the ground, just as Wade landed on top of him, forcing Plum to exhale at speed. Wade bounced back a little and banged his head on the steps.

'Gotcha!' Wade shouted as he laid his throbbing head backwards. Beneath him, Plum did not move. He would not be running or threatening for quite some time, especially as his head was wedged painfully between iron railings. Wade looked up and squinted. Above him, he could see that Faiza and Miss Corner were making their way down the spiral stairs towards him. He lay there, panting heavily. His head was spinning from the circular running and the sudden stop. Wade focused on the stairs above him; the ones he had just hurtled down. He squinted and then smiled. Then he let out a hearty, exhausted, happy laugh. He knew where the gold had been hidden.

43

'You stupid Squib! You could have been killed,' said Faiza, punching him in the arm as she bent over him a few moments later.

'Ha – beat you down!' he mumbled. They both smiled as she held his hand. He coughed lightly. 'I found the gold, Fize. I found where the gold is hidden!' he said but stopped as Miss Corner caught up and bent down next to them.

'Well, Kashive, or Wade, or whatever your name is, you were pretty stupid back there.' She frowned, then smiled. 'But personally, I think you deserve a medal. Nicely done.'

'Miss Corner,' said Faiza urgently. 'Is Jack ok? Our friend?' Miss Corner nodded.

'He's fine. Plum stupidly had him shipped to LPS house to hide him, but he's safe there. We'll all join him there shortly.' Two large gentlemen on the stairs below cast a shadow over them. 'Ah Three-seven and Four-five, can you take these two honoured guests to McCoy to have them medically checked over and then take them to LPS House. Look after them.' The two men acknowledged and helped take both Faiza and Wade to an ambulance outside.

Corner's expression changed, and she turned to Plum, who lay there semi-conscious. She pulled his head up slightly by his hair. He groaned a little as the railings pressed into his neck.

'Mr Plum. If we ever get you out of this self-imposed prison, you'll be dismissed and face charges of conspiracy to pervert the course of justice, theft, treason, misuse of CO8 property and you really, *really* hacked me off. She let his head go and it hit the concrete stair with a *clonk*.

Forty-five minutes later and they were all seated in Discussion Suite Four. This time however there were no blindfolds, harsh words or threats. Instead, there were drinks and food and happy conversation.

'Well, Faiza and Wade, your friend Jack will be here shortly. I think I've got all your names and details right this time and not a Starfleet captain in sight.' Miss Corner smiled. They heard the familiar click of the door and were overjoyed to see Jack come bounding through.

'Jack!' they both shouted in unison and had a group hug.

'I'm really pleased to see you,' he said in typical understatement.

'Mr Roble?' cut in Miss Corner. 'Pleased to meet you again. Before we start, would you like us to notify anyone you are here?' All three of them imagined how that conversation would go and the potential panic it would cause. Looking at each other, Wade spoke first.

'Erm, no. If it's ok, we'd rather explain things to our parents first, although it would help if you came along to back up our story!'

'I completely understand,' replied Miss Corner, shuffling her papers.

'Jack, I'm sorry that you got captured,' said Wade more quietly.

'S'okay, it was quite exciting really,' he replied. 'I hope that Mr Blue got his comeuppance!'

'You won't believe who he really is!' said Wade excitedly.

'And you even tried to put them off our trail. We owe you,' said Faiza in admiration. Jack nodded and was about to say they were all in it together, when another more important thought occurred.

'Wadey, did you find it? Did you get the gold?' blurted Jack, wide-eyed. Miss Corner stopped shuffling and looked over her glasses. Silently she mouthed the word *gold*. Wade smiled.

'You bet your SSD we found it!' laughed Wade, patting Jack's shoulder.

'Yes, yes we need to come to that. I heard you all talking at the top there about the missing gold – *Corner's Calamity* – is it true?' she said in her northern Irish accent.

'Miss Corner, my dear Miss Corner. We are about to make your day!' said Faiza beaming.

'Are you saying that Plum was right – this has a lot to do with the gold that went missing in the war? The gold my grandfather William Corner was hunting for?' she sounded very disbelieving.

'It's *everything* to do with the missing gold and we've found it. We did it!' Wade's voice grew louder and higher. Miss Corner looked at them and switched on the recording device.

'Tell me everything and don't leave out anything.' All three of them looked at each other, eager to tell their story.

'Can we have some of that food first – I'm starving!' said Wade. She nodded and the three of them began tucking in.

'So as I said, *tell me everything*. From the very start.'

Taking turns, in no particular order, they told the whole story. From Wade almost stumbling over the UXB in the park to the trip to the Imperial War Museum, the trip to Bank twice and getting into a hidden chamber. Then there was the sewer experience.

They told her exactly how they had managed to escape from Discussion Suite Four the first time – the firing range in the sub-basement and the escape into the old King William Street tunnels. When they got to the part of the tale of the old disused station that had the skeleton of Greengage and the old train, Miss Corner took more notes. They detailed the rest of their adventure, finally arriving at the Monument. Miss Corner took off her glasses and looked at them.

'That sounds incredulous and at this point I am full of awe and wonder at your ability to get yourselves in, and out of, dangerous and dirty situations. But look, amazing though this is, there is a part of me wondering whether you made all this up for that amazing creative writing competition…?' Collectively, they shook their heads.

'Sure, and I might just believe it… but you omitted the biggest detail of all.'

'Where the gold is now?' asked Wade, grabbing another piece of cake.

'Where the gold is right now,' she said, looking right at them.

44

Faiza looked at Wade who looked at Jack.

'Captain Quiet – this is your moment,' ushered Faiza to Jack.

'It's quite clever, but this is what we think happened,' said Jack. 'Plum senior knew the only way to keep the gold hidden was to hide it for a while and then move it.'

'Yes, I got that from what you said earlier, but where is it now?' she seemed a little terse.

'I was coming to that. He got it across the Thames and changed into his ghost outfit using some of his white paint and transported it close to the Monument.'

'The Monument? Well, I guessed that by where we found you and Plum, but where? The metal emblem on the top – he'd never have got it up there!' said Miss Corner.

'No. He got 311 small bricks and put them in plain sight,' explained Jack.

'Are you lot always like this?' asked Miss Corner, growing impatient.

'I'm afraid they are – a real geek squad. This isn't X-Factor – just tell her, will you!' replied Faiza crossly.

'They're under the stairs,' he explained. '311 small bars were painted white and welded to the underneath of each of the stairs in the Monument! It's ingenious. Sitting in plain sight, for over eighty years.' Jack sat back, with a pleased look on his face.

Miss Corner nodded and pressed a button on the desk. 'Did you get that, Miss Place? Send squad 6P and check it out.' She released the button and turned back to them. 'There anything else to add?' said Miss Corner excitedly.

'Well, the rest is history – Plum senior was greedy and so went back to check on his handiwork and maybe even take some of the gold and that's when he got blown up by a bomb in the Blitz! His other associate didn't know where he'd hidden it so died penniless,' Jack explained. Miss Corner smiled knowingly.

'If this is all true and we can prove it, you will have the thanks of the nation and my personal thanks.'

'Is there a reward?' asked Wade. Faiza elbowed him.

'Possibly, probably,' Miss Corner replied, smiling. 'The only nagging thing is – the 311 bars don't make the whole hoard. I wonder where the rest went to? Not important right now I guess. Maybe you can try and find the rest of it sometime!' She laughed and her three guests just looked shocked.

'Just joking. I'm off to see Plum soon. He'll be questioned and charged. Looks like he's brought his whole family into disrepute.'

'Oh, wait till people hear about our story!' said Wade excitedly.

'Yes, about that. Feel free to talk about what you did and even how you did it, but keep me, Plum and CO8 out of it. It may be difficult, but please don't mention details of this organisation or the people in it, especially agent three-nine; our Mr Plum,' Miss Corner said earnestly.

'Of course, we understand,' said Faiza, getting the nod from the others.

'In the meantime, we're going to get you home. My assistant – Miss Place – will accompany you to verify your story to your parents. I will be in touch soon. In the meantime, avoid tunnels,' she said, laughing.

'Can I finish this cake first?' asked Wade, spluttering crumbs onto the table.

45

For the first time ever, Wade and Faiza left for school together the next day.

'That was much better than I thought,' said Wade, once out of earshot of the house.

'Yeah, well we sure had a bit of explaining to do,' replied Faiza.

'I'm glad Miss Place was there too – I doubt they would have believed us otherwise! It was a good idea to leave out the bit about Mr Blue – erm, Plum!'

A long black car pulled alongside them and stopped. There was an electronic whirr as the back window wound down and Jack stuck his head out.

'Get in, get in!' he laughed, opening the door. They both got in the car to find Jack and Miss Corner in the back. This was no small car.

'Glad we found you. We called at your house, but you'd already left. Well, how are you today?' asked Miss Corner.

'Not bad. Are you taking us to school?' asked Faiza. Miss Corner nodded.

'Jack, how did it go?' asked Wade.

'Not bad, my dad was a bit cross at first, but then knew I'd done good!' said Jack smiling. 'How about you?'

'Good, good – Mum and Dad were more worried than anything else, I guess, but they knew we'd done good too. My dad did ask if there was a reward,' said Wade.

'Well let me give you an update on the case,' said Miss Corner earnestly. 'We investigated the gold and you'll be happy to hear, you were right. All the steps had a gold bar painted white attached to them. Within an hour we got 311 bars of the gold that had been missing for so long. There's still a lot missing though…' She let her voice trail off.

'Good news though; Plum has been detained indefinitely and will stand charges, as he is a member of the service, his trial will be in secret. But trust me, he won't be coming out for a long, long time.' There were some cheers as she said this.

The buildings, roads and even people they knew so well passed in a blur. 'I have more good news for you.' Again, she paused and waited.

'Well?' Wade eventually asked, growing impatient.

'See, not as funny as you think, that pausing thing, is it?' She and Faiza laughed.

'Firstly, Jack, your dad is going to find out some good news today. The increase in rent for this year has been cancelled and the rent for the next two years has been paid in advance. It should make things a little easier.' She smiled. Jack's eyes went a little glassy and his bottom lip appeared to quiver a little. He looked out of the window, unable to speak. Jack knew what this would mean to his dad and his family.

'Faiza and Wade? Good news for your mum and dad. We've been in touch with some authorities, and they've looked at the housing situation and have managed to find a larger home more suitable for a growing family. It's close to where you live now. The council will be in touch.' Corner smiled again, as Wade and Faiza managed a high-five.

'Oh, and the rent has been paid in advance for the next two years too.' It was Wade's turn to have a wobbly lip. 'But that's not the only good news – there is a substantial reward.' All three of them held their breath, as Miss Corner read out the prepared statement.

'For recovering over seven point eight million pounds in stolen gold bullion, Her Majesty's Government and Treasury would like to award Wade Carter, Faiza Saab and Jack Roble the sum of twenty-five thousand pounds.' The cheers made the windows vibrate!

'Oh erm – that's *each*,' she added, smiling.

They continued to cheer loudly as the car slowed and stopped at the end of a long line of traffic.

'Damn – is there a quicker way?' asked Miss Corner.

'Yes, I'll show you,' said Faiza eagerly. As she and Miss Corner leaned in to tell the driver the best way to school avoiding the traffic, Jack leaned into Wade and whispered.

'Wade – listen, don't say a word, but I did something!'

'What did you do?' Wade whispered back.

'It was me – I got an extra bar of gold.'

'What?' Wade remembered in time not to shout. 'How? what, really?' he whispered.

'Yeah – remember when we were in that spooky Underground station and the deserted train with the moulds and paint?'

'Yeah?'

'Well in amongst the paint, I found a bit of white metal. I thought it might be useful later, so I picked it up and pocketed it,' he beamed. 'It's actually gold! Do you reckon I should own up?'

'Are you kidding? Don't you dare! That's ours – erm – yours!' hissed Wade. Just then the others sat back from their driver instruction.

'What are you whispering about?' said Faiza suspiciously.

'Just wondering what to spend our money on,' said Wade. 'I was thinking of a one-way ticket to New Zealand for you.'

'Ah that's sweet, I'll get you one to the moon.' They both laughed. A few seconds later, the car rounded a corner and cruised into the school car park, stopping in the Head's parking space.

Many of the pupils from the school crowded round the dark-windowed car trying to see who the occupants were. The Head, Mr Crowther, looked out of his window and a few seconds later appeared at the doorway along with a few other curious teachers. The driver, a large burly man dressed in a black suit, got out and opened the door to let Wade, Faiza and Jack out. They all looked around to the cheers, and jeers, of their friends. Wade spotted Mrs Poppet next to the Head and said to her in a loud voice.

'Mrs Poppet, you won't believe what happened to me at the weekend!'

Epilogue

Four miles away in a room above a dimly-lit back alley, a man strolled between a table and his single bed. He held a mobile phone to his ear.

'Yes, I know, but what can I do about it? You blew it, Bro, you blew it,' he was saying as he walked. 'Wow, you've got a temper. Yeah, thanks to the press, we know a lot more now. We'll wait a while, then I'll go a-knocking.'

He continued for another minute and after ending the call, threw his phone on the bed. He looked around his bedsit and sighed. He took off his orange Hi-Viz vest and hung it on the back of the door. As he did so, he caught sight of his nameplate and squinted. There was some grit blocking out his surname. He scratched it with his thumb, revealing his full name. The name read '*Mr Tim Plum*'.

CPSIA information can be obtained
at www.ICGtesting.com
Printed in the USA
LVHW042201120722
723217LV00006B/252

9 781915 229212